Mary Stewart was one of the 20th century's bestselling and best-loved novelists. She was born in Sunderland, County Durham in 1916, but lived for most of her life in Scotland, a source of much inspiration for her writing. Her first novel, *Madam, Will You Talk?* was published in 1955 and marked the beginning of a long and acclaimed writing career. In 1971 she was awarded the International PEN Association's Frederick Niven Prize for *The Crystal Cave*, and in 1974 the Scottish Arts Council Award for one of her children's books, *Ludo and the Star Horse*. She was married to the Scottish geologist Frederick Stewart, and died in 2014.

Praise for Mary Stewart:

'She set the bench mark for pace, suspense and romance – with a great dollop of escapism as the icing.'

Elizabeth Buchan

'The world's leading romantic-suspense writer'

Sunday Times

'A comfortable chair and a Mary Stewart – total heaven. I'd rather read her than most other authors.'

Harriet Evans

MARY STEWART

The Wind Off the
Small Isles

and

The Lost One

With a foreword by
Jennifer Ogden

HODDER

First published in Great Britain in 1968 by Hodder & Stoughton
An Hachette UK company

This paperback edition published in 2017
by Hodder & Stoughton

1

A CIP catalogue record for this title is available from the British Library

Paperback ISBN 978 1 473 64125 9
Ebook ISBN 978 1 473 64123 5

Typeset in Plantin Light by Palimpsest Book Production Limited,
Falkirk, Stirlingshire

Printed and bound by CPI Group (UK) Ltd, Croydon, CR0 4YY

Hodder & Stoughton policy is to use papers that are natural, renewable and
recyclable products and made from wood grown in sustainable forests. The
logging and manufacturing processes are expected to conform to the
environmental regulations of the country of origin.

Hodder & Stoughton Ltd
Carmelite House
50 Victoria Embankment
London EC4Y 0DZ

www.hodder.co.uk

for
ANGELINE and ROBERT,
with love

Dear Reader,

The Wind Off the Small Isles is a perfect example of Mary Stewart's perfect writing.

In all of her novels, as with this one, Mary always travelled to where she was going to set her book. Whilst she was there, she would make copious and detailed notes in order that she always had everything in her scenes set correctly. The extraordinary descriptive power of her writing shows this to be the case. Nothing less would have done for her with this novella set on the island of Lanzarote.

Mary spent several holidays in the Canary Islands with her husband Fred, an eminent geologist and professor at Edinburgh University. It was a visit to Lanzarote – some part of which was spent clambering in and out of extinct volcanos! – that inspired this small volume. Fred had decided he needed Mary in his photos so that when he was using them in lectures he would be able to show his students how to gauge the size of the craters. Oh, the things she did for love. But just as much as these adventures, it was the local legends and the numerous and diverse numbers of wildflowers and the rugged, stark topography of this island which inspired her to set her story here. The title is really evocative of what it is like on Lanzarote: wild, beautiful and definitely windy.

As her niece and also her constant companion for the last twelve years of her life, I came to know Mary Stewart (Aunty Mary) extremely well and also to realise how lucky we have been as a family to have had within it this extraordinary and fascinating woman. I miss her terrific sense of humour, her flashes of brilliance, her kind heart and her generosity to everyone she met or knew. Most of all, though, I recall her love for us, her nieces and nephews. We took the place of the children she could never have. The memories of her visits when we were small are filled with scenes of a beautiful woman who always smelled heavenly (Chanel comes to mind now), who was exquisitely dressed and always came armed with presents.

I am sad there will never be another new Mary Stewart book, but the ones she wrote will stand the test of time to be read over and over again by new generations. It is so pleasing that this lovely, lost little book, *The Wind Off the Small Isles*, has finally been re-published, in time to celebrate what would have been Mary's one-hundredth birthday. I hope you enjoy reading it.

Jennifer Ogden
23 May 2016

The Wind Off the
Small Isles

Prelude

She knelt on the window-sill, looking out over the sea. The night was clear, with a faint moon rising, but the stars seemed dim and far away. It must be imagination, but they were not white tonight; the evening star had risen apricot-yellow, and now the main flock of stars crowded hazy and ill-defined above a horizon smoking with purple and cinnamon and grey. This was strange, for the day had been sharp and fine, with a sky settled to blue again after the eruption, and the wind blowing strongly from the north, straight from Cape Finisterre and the coast of Spain and down the chain of the Atlantic islands.

Anxiously she peered into the darkness. Yes, the wind blew still. On the wall of the goat-pen near the cliff's edge she could see the bougainvillaea tossing, and above the roof the palm-leaves shuffled and clicked like playing cards.

Her father had gone to bed long since. He had won tonight, and lying wakeful, waiting, she had heard him call a jovial '*Buenas noches*' after his friends. Then the heavy door had shut, and the men's footsteps, with the quick pattering of old Señor Perez' donkey, had dwindled up the lane into silence.

That was two hours since, and soon the moon would rise clear of the cactus slopes behind the house, and by its light she would see him coming.

Mother of God, let him come. He promised, and I know he is true. I know he will come. He promised.

The rosary moved in her fingers, but she was not praying. That time was over. This was now, the night itself, the night the prayers were to be answered. The clenched beads scored her fingers, and she shut her eyes. When she opened them again, he would be here, his boat stealing round the headland into the bay . . . Till then, she would shut her eyes on that empty sea, and think about him, as if by thinking she might make his coming sure.

Against the fizzing dark inside her eyelids she could see him now as she had first seen him three weeks ago, down there on the white sand of the bay, the muscles glancing and sliding under his brown skin as he braced himself in the shallows to pull his boat inshore. She had turned quickly away, as a modest girl should, but Conchita had run, child-like, down to the boat to peer in at the catch of fish. She had hesitated then, and called, but the child paid no attention, and then the young fisherman had turned, straightening, and smiled at her. He was barefooted, and his breeches were ragged, and faded with salt and sun, but the light ran and glinted on wet gold skin and black hair, and she could think of nothing but how the smile drove the deep crease down his cheek and lit the dark eyes . . . Then the smile had gone, and he was staring, and she had stood with her eyes on his and her heart choking her, till Conchita had run back, laughing, and pulled at her hand.

She opened her eyes, and he was here. Round the north headland, shadowy on the shadowy sea, the boat stole like a night-bird, under sail. She thought she could even see him, a shape at the tiller, dark against the sea-fire as the boat heeled in the gentle curve that would bring him into the bay.

She left the sill and moved over to the bed. Her sister's breathing was so quiet that it hardly stirred the air. She hesitated, stooping over the bed, the rosary dangling from her hand, its tiny cross swinging on a silver link. She tugged at this, and the link parted, and she dropped the cross, warm from her skin, on the child's pillow. Then she picked up the bundle of clothes wrapped in her shawl, and paused with a hand on the door. A cloud, thick and dark, drove past the window, but she did not need light to show her the room in whose familiar safety she had slept every night of her eighteen years – the bed of Canary pine, the coffer with its worn oak carving that had been her great-grandmother's dower chest, the wrought-iron candlesticks, the crucifix on the wall: they had been here all her life, they had spelled safety and love. Now she would spell love her own way. And safety, too . . .? Mary Mother, but she must believe what her heart told her, and soon she would be sure . . .

She slipped out through the door and along the flagged passage to the kitchen. The dog raised his head and blinked at her, and his tail thumped briefly. The wind blew strongly, and in the draught the straw mats rose along the flagstones.

Something drove rattling against the window-panes, like a handful of rain. The moon's light had gone, and now she saw how the dark clouds smoked across the stars. Against them, suddenly, light beat redly, and was gone. Then she smelt the faint, familiar reek, and knew the clouds, the sleet, for what they were: the ash-cone to the north, the little Loma, had woken again and was throwing out more ash and cinders. And the wind blew from there.

She checked, while beside her the dog flattened his ears, and his ruff stirred. If she called now to wake them . . . La Loma was harmless; all it had done last week – all it ever did – was to shower the place with ashes, and singe a field or two . . . Ten minutes, and the boat could be clear of the island and beyond pursuit . . . But call them she must. She could not go like this, leaving them asleep . . .

As she turned back from the door, she felt the air move like blast, and round the door the light pulsed red, then died to black again. The dog's chain rattled; he whined, then began to bark, furiously. Somewhere a door slammed, and she heard her father's voice. They were awake. She pulled open the heavy door as the night lit once more with an arched jet of fire, and the smell of blown sulphur rolled over the yard. A gull went up from the roof, screaming, and as she ran past the pens she heard the beasts bleating with fear.

Her father called out again, and she saw her bedroom window flower with light as he ran in with the lamp. Her sister's voice answered, shrill and startled. The light sharpened suddenly as he approached the window. The pane was thrust open, and the light spilled out to catch her where she stood, pinned against the outhouses like a moth.

She saw the big head thrust out, peering past the flame. The night was black again. The mountain held its breath. But he saw her. He shouted, 'It'll be no more than last time. Let them bide, but see the windows are boarded. Then get yourself to the cellar with your sister.'

The casement shut. The lamp withdrew. As she put a hand, dutifully, to the gaps that served the pens for windows, the mountain shot out a plume of fire that lit the night and showed her the boards fast in their places. She turned and ran across the yard and down the cliff path.

He was there. He was waiting for her below the cactus slopes, as he had said he would wait. He had his best suit on, and a cloak made of coarse blanket, and he was bareheaded.

He put his arms out for her and she ran into them.

I

Stolen to this paradise.

KEATS: *The Eve of St Agnes*

My employer, Cora Gresham, is a woman of wealth, and also a woman of whims. She is a writer of children's stories, anything from riproaring adventure to animal cartoons and space fiction, and has the habit of using exotic and authentic backgrounds for what she calls their educational value. In consequence she is liable to set off for the most out-of-the-way corners of the world at a moment's notice, and the life of her secretary and personal assistant – myself – is by no means a dull one.

It came as no surprise, therefore, when it was the turn of a new 'Coralie Gray' adventure about pirates along the Barbary Coast, to be told to get things in train – and that within a matter of days – for a visit to the Canary Islands.

This was my fault, if fault it can be called. I had had to do all the preliminary research; I had combed through loads of books from the library, haunted travel agents and pestered the air lines, and then presented Mrs Gresham with glowing and wildly enthusiastic descriptions of the islands which from time out of mind have been known as the Fortunate Isles or the Isles of the Blessed, and which, we are told, were the original Garden of the Hesperides.

And if there weren't still nymphs and golden apples, I told her, there were still dragon trees, and the great Mount Teide, twelve thousand feet high and crowned with snow, and for all we know with Atlas still up there on his shoulders, carrying the sky. There were warm indigo seas lapping on black lava beaches, and aquamarine seas lapping on white beaches, and everywhere flowers and bright birds and perpetual summer . . . I don't think she was even listening. She sat looking at a map of the Canary archipelago, while outside the windows the northern English rain beat solidly down on the brave, soaked daffodils of March. Then she put a finger on the map.

'That one,' she said.

'Lanzarote? But you can't possibly – weren't you even listening? That's the one I told you was practically a desert! It's all volcanic ash, and the book says it's like a lunar landscape or something from another world. Heavens, they filmed *Two Thousand Years before Christ* there, and I'm told it looks like it!' I drew in my breath. 'What's more, there's a great chain of volcanoes called the Fire Mountains, still hot and active, and probably going off at any minute—'

'It's the one nearest Africa,' said Mrs Gresham.

'I dare say it is, but your pirates could just as easily get from the Barbary Coast through to Grand Canary, or Tenerife, and either of those would make a perfectly gorgeous setting.'

'Probably, but I've been looking at the references you gave me, and it seems to have been Lanzarote they usually got to first. Look here at the map and you'll see why. The point is that, apart from all the landings recorded – and there were a good many – there must have been dozens of small raids going on all the time, so anything I like to invent can fit in very well.'

'Yes, but does that actually matter?' I looked over her shoulder. 'There must have been raids on the other islands, and you see how the Barbary Coast lies north of the Canaries, so if your pirates cast just a little further west they'd have missed Lanzarote and the other dry island – what's it called? Fuertaventura – and come on the fertile islands in the westerly group.' I ran my finger down the map. 'That way.'

'I see that, but I think it really will have to be Lanzarote. It fits my story too well.' She tapped the pile of books beside her. 'You remember that I want my pirates to run an expedition to recover some of their friends taken in the slave raids? Well, the Counts of Lanzarote seem to have done a tremendous amount of slaving along the African coast. In fact, I thought I might even use a genuine return raid, the one some time in the 1580s when the Countess of Lanzarote had to hide in that cave under the lava beds. I forget where you put the notes.'

'They're here. Yes, the Cueva De Los Verdes. All right, I give in. It would be rather good, I see that. I'll put it down as a "must" for us to explore.'

'I'm sorry you won't see Teide and your dragon trees,' said Mrs Gresham. 'Some other time, I hope. And I'm sure Lanzarote can't be as bad as you make out. It's even coming on to the tourist route now, isn't it? It wouldn't do that if there wasn't something to be said for it. At least one person I know – James Blair, as it happens, and my younger son was with him – spent a few weeks there getting over the flu last year, and I remember reading something he wrote about it. He loved it. He called it "the last paradise". Of course Michael raved about it, but that's nothing to go by, all he thinks about is swimming.'

'I'm rather that way myself. Ah, well, at least it will be

different. Though as for "paradise" – I suppose it's all in the mind. According to the pictures there are no trees, and they have to make special holes in the volcanic ash to grow their fruit, and there'll be no flowers worth mentioning because it only rains about two days in the year.'

'And that,' said my employer, closing the atlas with a snap, 'settles it. We go there. Fix it up, will you?'

There is one thing about Mrs Gresham, when she has made a decision she sticks by it. Now that she had decided on Lanzarote, she would find it delightful, or die in the attempt. So when precisely ten days after the conversation (in my own way I am as efficient as Coralie Gray) she surveyed the strange, windy landscape of Lanzarote and exclaimed, 'But Perdita, it's beautiful!' I was not surprised. What did surprise me was that I found myself agreeing with her.

The island was every bit as wild and barren as I had imagined. The roads stretched, pitted and dusty, between ridges of black basaltic lava. The only tree was an occasional palm, the only hills the symmetrical cones of dead volcanoes, or, to the south, the great burnt ridges of the Fire Mountains, with the frozen black floods of lava filling the valleys between them. There was no grass. There were no woods. The villages were pure African – square flat-roofed houses painted white and ochre, set flat like little boxes on the baked earth. Above them, where one looked for minarets, the towers of the Spanish churches looked incongruous and foreign.

Strange and exciting, you would have thought, rather than beautiful. 'Paradise' – no, never. But then it got you. You stopped the car on some deserted track they called a road, and got out into the silent afternoon, the thick dust muffling even the sound of your footsteps. You stood looking at the long, yellow fields, with their pattern of growing corn like ribbed velvet, the soot-black slopes honey-combed with pits each enclosing a fig tree in brilliant green bud, the burning range of volcanic mountains shouldering up in great sweeps of red against the dazzling sky . . . all these made a tranquil and somehow intensely satisfying pattern of shape and colour in the pure air. It was beauty more than naked; beauty pared to the bone. And always there was the wind. Cool and steady, the trade wind – 'tracked wind' – funnelled its way down through the small outlying islands to overleap these dry eastern isles and drop its rain on the flowers and green forests of Tenerife and Grand Canary.

It was on our second day in Lanzarote that Mrs Gresham decided that she would buy a house there.

'It really is the perfect retreat,' she told me. '"Paradise" was true enough, if by that you mean something out of this world. Just think of the peace and quiet, think of the sunshine, think of being able to get all the help in the house you want without having to worry about it.'

'Think of being nearly two thousand miles away from home. Think of the Canary telephone system. Think of having your mail all opened and read. Think of not knowing a single word of Spanish except *mañana* and *hasta la vista*,' I said. 'Besides, I'd leave you. You know perfectly well you couldn't do a thing without me. I practically write your books as it is.'

'Dear child, I know. But you'd love it, you really would. It isn't as if it would be for ever, just a year or two—'

'A *year* or two? Now, look—'

'What's a year to you? You can spare it better than I can, after all. No, I'm serious. This might be the place really to pause and take stock of oneself, and maybe write something worth while.'

'Everything you write is worth while,' I said, promptly and firmly. I knew this mood. Mrs Gresham, who is nothing if not clear-sighted, once called herself 'the clown with the normal clown's urge to play Hamlet', but this didn't seem to me to fill the bill. I called it her 'Sullivan act' – a finished master of light music breaking his heart to be Verdi. I said: 'I wish you'd stop tormenting yourself because you're not Graham Greene or James Blair or Robert Bolt or someone. The number of people who'd miss "Coralie Gray" if you stopped writing could be laid end to end—'

'I know, I know. It's all right, you don't need to hold my hand today. That's one reason why I think I would like to stay in this place, even if it's only for a few months – there really is peace here, and yet not a relaxing peace. Tranquillity's the word. One would be hedged in by quiet-ness, and I think one could write. Look over there, nothing but sea and sky and wind and the small islands . . .'

We were sitting – we had been picnicking – on the northernmost point of the island, the Bateria del Rio, where a high cape rears a windy head of red cliff some fifteen hundred feet above the blue slash which is the strait between Lanzarote and the white island of Graciosa. Graciosa is white because it consists entirely of sand, save for the grey cones of its three dead volcanoes. Beyond these ghostly pyramids, more dimly, floated the shapes of the other islands.

'Even their names,' said Mrs Gresham. 'The Pleasing Isle, the Isle of Rejoicing, the Clear Mountain, the Eagle's Rock—'

'You're surely not thinking of living *there*!'

'No, that's a little bit too peaceful, even for me. I'd go round the bend in a week, and what you'd do I hate to think.' She shivered suddenly and pulled her coat round her. 'And the wind. I don't like the wind.'

'Don't you? I love it.'

'You're young. When you're my age you'll find that "the wind on the heath, brother," is only good for rheumatism and damaging the garden. Come back to the car. We'll go home the other way, and see if we can find somewhere sheltered.'

I picked up the picnic things. 'There's always the Cueva De Los Verdes, where your Countess hid out during the raid. Do you want to visit that this afternoon? I think we go right by it.'

We found the signpost – a rather chichi affair of polished rustic work and antique lettering – which pointed the way off into a plain of tumbled black lava, but when we had bumped our way hopefully along the appalling track, the only 'cave' we could find was a large gaping depression in the lava, more like a quarry than a cave. It looked as if the top crust of solidified lava had collapsed, exposing a section of an underground tunnel which ran into darkness under the sharp and overhanging edges of the hole. We looked at it without enthusiasm.

'Well, that's it,' I said. 'Even if you could get in; it simply wouldn't be safe without a guide. What do you say I fix it up and bring you back another day?'

'And that would let you out?' She laughed. 'All right. Go and turn the car while I take a look round the top.'

It was quite a relief to be back on what the maps were pleased to call the main road. Some way further on, right in the middle of the lava plain which stretches along the north-east coast, we saw the notice sticking up: 'Plots for Sale.'

It was about as reasonable as seeing 'Good Building Land' advertised in the middle of the Solway mudflats. This was old lava, from long-ago eruptions, nothing more nor less than a plain of dusty, broken black rock with cutting edges, lightened here and there by the brilliant yellow-green sponges of some succulent, and the phalli of the candelabra cactus, like clustered stands of organ-pipes acid with verdigris. Nothing else grew. As building land it was ludicrous. The only way one could live there was to buy one of the caves that gaped here and there in the lava – monstrous holes disappearing into blackness – and set up house in that.

'Cheaper, too,' I said. 'Look, if you want to use a cave for your story, why don't we just go to the Jameos del Agua? It's another cave near here, and they've turned it into a restaurant, so at least it should be easy to get into. It shouldn't be far away – in fact, isn't that a signpost a bit further along the road, to the left?'

'It looks like it. Well, if you like. Do you suppose they'd run to a cup of tea?'

'I'm sure they would.'

'Then *vamos*,' said my employer.

But the signpost did not mention the Jameos del Agua. It was merely a board, weathered white by sun and the salt wind, on which had been roughly painted the words *Playa Blanca*.

'Doesn't that mean white beach?' asked Mrs Gresham. 'If it's like those lovely beaches in the south there might be a café—'

'I'm sure there won't be. This isn't the tourist end of the island – I mean, you can see why, can't you? And that's not a touristy kind of notice, it's too shabby and genuine. If it leads anywhere at all apart from the beach, it'll just be to a farm or something.'

'Go down, anyway, and let's have a look.'

'I thought you were dying for some tea?'

'There might be something there. In any case, we've still got some wine left over from lunch, haven't we? And if it is a white beach you can have a swim.'

'This being the one day I haven't brought my swimming things.'

'It mightn't matter, at that. Go on, it would be lovely to find a quiet place right out of the wind, and the shore down there's bound to be sheltered. We'll probably find we've got it all to ourselves.'

'I wouldn't be surprised,' I said grimly, as I put the car in gear and turned it off the road into a horrible track that plunged down at right-angles through the lava bed. It was like driving through a coal tip. The black dust was at least six inches deep, and the wheels churned and skidded through it, every now and again jerking across hunks and ruts of broken lava, so sharp that I was in constant terror for my tyres. The track became a lane, deep between lava walls crowned with the candelabra cactus, which after a while gave way to a sort of jungle of prickly pear, so thickly grown that not even a goat could have pushed its way through. We ploughed steeply downwards, trailing our wake of black dust.

'I only hope if we do get down that there's a place to turn,' I said.

'It must go somewhere. After all, there was a signpost.'

'It might only be to a beach. If I've got to turn on sand—'

'You could reverse up.'

'You've got to be joking.' We bucketed round a bend between the monstrous cactus hedges. 'Thank heaven for that! There's a farm or something, there's bound to be a gate where I can turn. Look, we really will have to stop here, I'm afraid. I daren't go further. Any minute now one of these tyres will go phut, and then we really will have to spend the night in a cave. It isn't far to the sea from here, we can walk down. I'll manage the picnic things.'

In fact the farm gate, set back to our right, marked the end of the track. Beyond the gate this dwindled merely to a path for goats, which wound its way even more steeply downwards for twenty yards or so, then branched off to zigzag down the shallow cliff towards the glimpse of white sand and sea.

I stopped the car between the stone gateposts. 'I'll have to drive right in to turn. We'd better ask them.'

'Drive in first,' said Mrs Gresham reasonably, 'then they can't stop you, can they? Besides, you've got to leave the car somewhere, and they might let you leave it in the yard.'

'You've got a point there.'

Inside the yard was the usual clutter one associates with a peasant's smallholding – a wood-stack, buckets, what looked like a galvanised-iron trough. I only vaguely saw them as I turned the car carefully in between the gateposts and manœuvred to turn. But beside me I heard Mrs Gresham make some sort of subdued exclamation, then she said, sharply for her: 'Look. Just look at that.'

It was certainly very picturesque. The house was single-storeyed, low and flat-roofed, with a 'picture' window facing the sea, and a garnet-red bougainvillaea tumbling over a whitewashed wall. Behind the house was the big beehive shape of a primitive oven, with the wood stacked beside it. Between the long front of the house and the edge of the low cliff there had obviously been at one time a sprawl of buildings; sheds and sties roughly built of mudbrick and undressed stone. These now lay tumbled into piles of rubble. Masonry and wood lay everywhere, and I realised that the trough and the buckets I had noticed were not farm implements at all, but builders' tools, and that there were no animals about, nor any signs of them. Now that I came to look at it, the house itself, with its new whitewash and the modern window, looked too sophisticated to be one of the primitive farmsteads we had seen elsewhere.

I knew what Mrs Gresham was going to say, and she said it. 'My house. This is it. No wonder my Daemon gave me a nudge and told me to come down here. This is my house, Perdita. Look at it. All we'd have to do is knock down the rest of these old sheds in front and floor the yard to make a terrace, and look at the view we'd have. Straight out of that window – the sea, and that flash of white sand at the bottom, and those black cliffs reaching up with their arms holding the bay. And not a living soul.'

'Well, somebody owns it,' I pointed out.

'Indeed yes, and now's as good a time as any to look for them and ask about it. You can do it. No, don't gape at me like that, my child. Switch the engine off and go and knock on the door.'

'Me? Why me?'

'Because I'm fat and fifty, and you're twenty-three and a dish,' said my employer frankly. 'You'll at least get a hearing, where I might not.'

'A hearing? And what do I use for Spanish?'

'Anything you like. If they're Spanish all you have to do is smile at them and they'd listen even if you talked Gobbledegook.'

'Well, thanks, but—'

'Now stop arguing, and go and see who lives there. They might speak a bit of English anyway, and at the very least you can probably find the name of the owners. Then when we get back to Arrecife we can make enquiries, and get a lawyer to take over from there. Go on, I'll wait in the car.'

I got out resignedly, and picked my way across the yard to the door, which was set deep in an archway in the end wall of the house. It was a thick, studded affair of heavy planking, which had recently been given a lick of blue paint. If it had been any use arguing with my employer, I would have pointed out that the new paint, and the evidence of building operations, suggested that someone had recently moved in and was doing on his own account just the improvements she had suggested, but I knew from experience that Mrs Gresham's impulses had to be allowed to wear themselves out in their own time, so I merely lifted a hand and knocked at the door.

The wood must have been very thick. The sound seemed to drown, almost, in the door itself. No echo. It was like knocking on a solid wall instead of a hollow door.

I waited for a bit, then tried again. Still no answer. But when I turned away, half in relief, Mrs Gresham called from the car:

'I can hear something round the other side. Someone talking, I think. Go round the front, I think they're at the far end.' And she waved towards a grove of palm trees and some softer green which showed beyond the house.

I went. At least it would be shady, and it was pleasant to be out of the car. It was mid-afternoon now, and the sun was hot, but a small breeze wandered even here, clicking the leaves of the palm trees. These made a grove of shade where a small patio had been newly laid out at the far end of the house and out of sight of the entrance yard. The patio, facing the sea, was enclosed on its three landward sides by the wall of the house, by the slope of black lava which rose steeply behind the house and was formidably overgrown with prickly pear, and by a black wall – now grey with builders' dust – where a gap made a gateway to the cliff top. In the shade of the palms stood a white painted metal table with a chair drawn up to it, and two or three brightly coloured beach chairs.

There was no one there. But a portable typewriter stood on the table with a pile of paper beside it weighted down by a rose-coloured shell. On the top page I could see a line of typing which looked like a title: *The Wind Off The Small Isles*.

'*Señorita?*'

A man's voice, sharp. I jumped and turned.

He was standing in the gap which opened on the cliff top. I hadn't heard or seen him coming, and now I saw why. Beyond the wall a small clump of tamarisk trees waved their frothy green at the cliff's edge, and in their light shade two men lay dozing, hats tipped over their eyes. Beside them was the remains of their meal, and a little further off some shovels, buckets and piles of what looked like sand and lime. They seemed to have been building a kind of low retaining wall along the edge of the cliff. It was their voices which Mrs Gresham must have heard, and now I had interrupted their siesta.

The man who had spoken was evidently some kind of foreman, for where the other two wore patched and dirty khaki trousers and the floppy straw island hats, and apparently worked stripped to the waist, this man had on a pair of reasonably decent blue denims and a short-sleeved shirt open at the neck. He was bareheaded.

'*Perdóneme,*' I said. '*Buenas tardes, Señor.*'

'"*Tardes.*' He was unsmiling, but this didn't mean

anything. Spain is not, like Italy, a land of flashing teeth and ready hands. He waited for me to explain myself.

'*Por favor, Señor*—' But here my Spanish ran out. At the sound of my voice the other two had roused themselves, and were sitting up, staring. I tried the smile that Mrs Gresham had recommended. 'Excuse me, but do you speak English?'

'Yes.' I thought there was something wary about the admission, as if he wasn't quite sure what it was going to let him in for. He was much younger than the other two. 'Can I help you?'

'It's only – my friend and I were driving down from El Rio and we saw the signpost and came down this little road to see what there was, and she . . . well, we couldn't turn the car, so we drove into the yard. I hope you don't mind?'

'Not at all. You wish me to turn it for you?'

'Oh, I can manage, thanks. It isn't that. My friend . . . as a matter of fact she's my employer . . . she sent me to ask what this house was and who owned it. I did knock at the door, but no one answered. I suppose it's a bad time to choose, siesta time? I'm sorry if I'm intruding.'

'There is no one at home.' He said no more, just waited there in the gap of the wall. If I was to find out anything at all I was going to have to persist. Perhaps he hadn't understood my rapid English. I spoke more slowly:

'Then perhaps you would just tell me – is the house itself called Playa Blanca, or is that the name of the beach?'

'It's the name of the beach, but the house goes by that name too. It's the only one here.'

The sun was making me blink. I moved a pace into shadow, narrowing my eyes at him. 'Surely you're English?' His eyes were hazel, not dark as I had thought. 'Is it your house, then?'

'No.'

I am not by nature aggressive and persistent, but since these are qualities which Cora Gresham values in her secretary, I persisted. 'But you speak it so well, *Señor* . . . Now I won't interrupt you any more, but I wonder if you'd just give me the name of the owner, please? That's really what my employer sent me to ask.'

I thought he hesitated. The other two men were on their feet now, staring at us, and he gestured irritably to them with some phrase in Spanish and a glance at his watch. As they trudged off to their buckets and cement, he turned back to me. 'I'm afraid I don't know. I only work here.' There was in fact, I noticed now, a faintly discernible Spanish accent. 'We are employed by an agent in Arrecife. Now we turn your car, eh?'

He crossed the patio, and with a gesture invited me to precede him back to the car. We walked together along the house-front.

'An agent in Arrecife?' I said. 'Then if you would be kind enough to give me his name? Just for the record, you know.'

'*Qué?*'

I stopped dead and turned. A hoopoe, startled, shot off a ruinous pigsty with a flare of camellia-rose and brilliant barred wings. Beyond it the sea flashed and glittered. The silence was profound.

I faced him squarely. 'Look, I'm sorry, but it's as much as my job's worth to let you push me right out without getting some kind of answer. And don't pretend you don't understand what I'm saying, because your Spanish accent's only just descended on you like Elijah's mantle. You are English, aren't you? And you've probably only just moved in, which is what it looks like, and you don't want to be bothered answering a lot of questions from someone who's obviously interested in the property? Fair enough, you wouldn't dream of selling – then all you have to do is say so. But wouldn't it be just as easy to tell me the name of your lawyer in Arrecife and let him do it for you? Straight up, it's as much as my job's worth to go back to the car now and tell my employer I haven't found out a thing about it. What's more, it's the quickest way of bringing her down on your neck that I've ever known. Just give me chapter and verse, and I'll clear us both straight out of your life and never come back.'

He grinned. It made him seem all at once much younger. 'That'd be a bit rough when I've only just met you, but if you want the truth, it's as much as *my* job's worth to tell you.'

No trace of Spanish accent now. I regarded him curiously. 'Top secret stuff? You mean you've actually had instructions not to tell?'

'Yes.'

'I'm right, they have just bought it? English?'

'Yes.'

'Well, that lets us both out, doesn't it? Relations of yours, parents?'

'No. I'm just assistant, looker-upper, apprentice, architect, watchdog, chauffeur and quite often keeper. But I'll tell you this, there isn't a chance in a million that my employer would dream of selling. This is his idea of the perfect hideout. I'm supposed to guard the gate like Cerberus and stop everyone coming in except the girl who brings the milk. Hence the strongarm stuff, for which I apologise, but orders is orders.' He waved a hand to the emptiness in front of us. 'He sounds like a wanted criminal, but he's not. All he wants is peace, and he thinks he's found it here.'

'Then this is where I came in. That's what my employer says, too, and what's more, your job sounds very much the same as mine – p.a., chauffeur, dog, devil and dairy-maid, and whatever you call the person who is sent out in front to draw the fire. As now.' I turned away. 'All right, if you've had your orders, this is something she will understand. They're two of a kind.'

'Mine's a writer,' he said apologetically, 'and more or less mad north-north-west.'

'I was busy guessing that. So's mine. That's what I meant. I don't mean she's mad – I must admit she's perfectly sane – but I see what you mean for all that.' I paused. 'Well, I'm sorry to have bothered you. Don't come any further, or you'll have to turn Spanish again. I can manage the car quite easily. Goodbye.'

'Half a minute, don't go yet – look, it's not my fault I've had to clam up like this, so won't you make it good for evil and tell me your name? Where are you staying? The hotel in Arrecife?'

'Yes. But I reckon I don't owe you my name.'

'Have a heart, I'll tell you mine. It's Mike, short for Michael—'

'*Michael!*'

We both jumped and spun round. Mrs Gresham was standing at the corner of the house, and as we both gaped at her, she screeched again: 'Michael!'

'For crying out loud.' There was more surprise than ecstasy in the young man's voice, but he advanced to meet her, and submitted cheerfully as she folded him to her.

Over her head he grinned at me. 'Well, what do you know? It's Mum. No wonder you said your employer needed a keeper.'

Mrs Gresham released him. '*Did* she?'

'Actually, she didn't. That was me.'

'If there's one straitjacket I covet more than another,' said Mrs Gresham, 'it's James Blair's. Perdita, as you'll have gathered, this is my son Michael.'

'I – is it? I mean, yes, we've met. I was just getting my breath back. So it's James Blair who lives here? I'm afraid he's beaten you to it, Mrs Gresham. He's just bought the house, and he's not parting.'

'You've seen him?'

'I have not. Your son said he was out, though I have no means of knowing whether that was the truth, but when you happened along I was being thrown out neck and crop, if that's the right expression, and you were to go too, but if he's your son he can't very well now, can he?'

'Certainly not. He's going to entertain us to tea,' said my employer, leading the way smartly towards the chairs under the palm-trees.

2

Ay, ages long ago
These lovers fled away . . .

KEATS: *The Eve of St Agnes*

'Well, now, Mike,' said Mrs Gresham, settling herself comfortably, 'what's all this about? I thought you were in Morocco.'

'Oh, we were. But ever since we stayed here before – in Lanzarote, I mean, the time he had flu and wanted to recoup so that he could finish *Tiger Tiger* for Julian Gale – he's talked about getting a place here as a bolt-hole.'

'I know. He told me about it.'

'Well, he'd asked an agent in Arrecife to keep his eyes open and report if anything suitable became vacant, and a couple of months ago it did. So here we are, moving in.'

It was coming straight now. The younger of Mrs Gresham's two sons had ambitions himself to be a playwright, and a year or two ago had, so to speak, apprenticed himself as research assistant and jack-of-all-trades to James Blair, one of our leading playwrights and a friend of the family. I had gathered from Michael's mother that learning, rather than earning, was the object of the job, and from the rare letters she had received it seemed that her son was enjoying himself hugely, the periods of gruelling work no less than the fallow intervals of travel and study. '*Michael was with him at the time, and raved about the swimming . . .*' That was probably the letter she had had at Christmas, written from Morocco, and I knew there hadn't been one since. Well, since I gathered that James Blair worked his assistant as hard as Cora Gresham worked me, Michael Gresham wouldn't write letters unless he had to. Few men did. Nor had he been home since I had been with his mother, so I had never met him, but now that I came to look at him, I could recognise through the dust and dishevelment the Mike Gresham of the younger photograph which stood in his mother's study; dark-brown hair, hazel eyes, a face that would have been undistinguished except for its shrewdness and humour and (what the photograph didn't show) the attractive crease that his sudden smile drove down his cheek.

He was smiling now. 'Look, do you really want tea? Won't you make it wine? It'll come up good and cold from the cellars. We're right over a nice holey hunk of lava here, and we've a genuine *cave*. Yes?'

He vanished into the house, from which he presently emerged carrying a tray with glasses, ice, olives and a bottle of the pale local wine called Chimidas. He set these down on the table, moving the papers on to a chair to make room.

'I know one's not allowed to notice something that's only half done,' I said, 'but is that his? Another play?'

'We hope so.' He began to pour the drinks. 'Only in the thinking stage as yet, and snag-ridden as usual. Ice? Try some soda, it sounds disgusting, but it makes a long cold drink with a mild sparkle, very refreshing when you're hot. There. Like it?'

I accepted the long misty glass, and sipped. 'Mm – yes, it's rather good.'

'My own invention.' Then he turned to his mother, and the two of them plunged into a rapid exchange of news, from which I gathered that Michael liked the job very much, and that he didn't expect the Canary Islands phase to outlast the writing of the play. 'Though goodness knows how long that will be. He's been going through a bad period, a more or less complete block since he got *Tiger Tiger* off his desk. If it's been anything like as trying for him as it has been for me—' He grimaced. 'Still, we may be through it now. Down in the forest something stirs. He's prowling round and round a new theme, so here's hoping.' He raised his glass, drank, and smiled at me. 'Do you go through this with my mother?'

I shook my head. 'Didn't you know? When she's stuck I just write them for her.'

'These rarefied agonies are not for me, thank heaven,' said Mrs Gresham. 'So he plans to stay here till it's finished? That could be a long time. What about you?'

'Oh, that's what he says,' said Michael, 'but you know what he's like, restless as the devil, and uses up about as much energy in a day as keeps most people going for a week. We'll no sooner get the place straight than he'll be fretting for London again. Not that I'm grumbling. I'm all for change myself, and let's face it, there are certain obvious lacks in this paradise of his. Or were . . . Well, Mother, it's your turn. What on earth brings you to Lanzarote?'

'Pirates,' said his mother concisely.

'Not Barbary Bill again? I thought you killed him off at the end of *Coast of the Corsairs*.'

'Dear boy, I can't afford to kill off my best-selling buccaneer. Reports of his death were found to be much exaggerated.' She set down her empty glass. 'No, no more, thank you. It was delightful. Now, Perdita and I are staying at the hotel in Arrecife, so the next time you can get off the chain, come and have dinner. Now we'll go. I don't want James to come back and find us here; I know how I feel about being interrupted myself. Give him my regards and tell him he'd be welcome, too, if he feels like an evening out.'

'For goodness' sake, don't go, he won't mind *you*,' said Michael. 'Some interruptions he minds, and some he doesn't. I mean it; do stay. I know he'll be pleased to see you, and you might think of me, marooned here all this time with only the workmen and my revered employer for company! In any case, work's over for the day . . . His, that is. Mine goes on.' He gestured, not to the typewriter, but to the workmen busy along the cliff.

'Good heavens,' said his mother, apparently seeing them for the first time. 'What are you doing over there?'

'Saving money and labour. As we demolish the goat-pens or whatever they are, we carry the stones along and use them for the retaining wall.'

'Will it be safe? It's very near the edge.'

'It's safe enough where the house is, never fear. I'm not so sure about the sides of the bay, but this centre part is solid. We're taking the retaining wall a little way along there to the right . . . Over that way there are one or two cracks in the surface lava, but they only go a short way down, and later eruptions obligingly filled them up with volcanic ash.'

'I see,' said his mother drily. 'I was wondering what you'd been doing to your clothes. He interprets "assistant" pretty liberally.'

Michael laughed. 'I enjoy it.'

'That I can see. You surely haven't done the alterations to the house yourself?'

'Oh, no, a real builder made the window, and rebuilt the main fireplace and made the kitchen usable, then he looked at the rest of the job and sold us his advice and the materials. Actually it looks as if we're doing an awful lot, but all that we've done ourselves is pull down the outhouses. They were just about derelict anyway. The builder comes and takes a look at us now and again, and his lads know their stuff . . . Everyone on this island seems to know all there is to know about working with stone. Have you seen the way they terrace the slopes?'

He had turned to me with the question, but before I could reply he looked quickly past me towards the house.

'What is it?' asked his mother.

I knew already. While he had been speaking I had heard the sound of a car bucketing down the horrible little lane. Now a door slammed, rapid footsteps crossed the yard, and James Blair came round the corner of the house.

I knew him from his photographs, of course. One's first impression of the famous playwright was that he looked very like Beethoven. He was a smallish man with deep-set eyes, a wild bush of hair, and a quiet manner which seemed to hide immense reserves of nervous energy. His voice was deep and rather harsh, and he occasionally hung on a word in a way that suggested a stammer overcome. It was only after some time that you realised he was shy.

He stopped dead when he saw us. Michael got to his feet. Mrs Gresham said:

'Well, James!'

James Blair's face changed. 'Cora Gresham! Well, well . . .' He came forward and met her outstretched hand. His look of pleasure was obviously genuine. 'Looking Mike up? He gave me away, then?'

'Not a word. It's pure accident that we came across

him, believe it or not. This is one of those coincidences that nobody would believe if you or I put it into print – at least, if you did they'd say it was a subtle denial of causality, and if I did they'd say it was romantic nonsense . . . James, this is Perdita West, who writes all my books and protects me from the world, presumably as Mike does for you.'

We murmured greetings, and shook hands. Mike said, grinning: 'Let's hope she's a bit more efficient at it than I am, letting my mother loose on you like this. I'm sorry, James.'

'From what I know of your mother, whom I esteem dearly,' said Mr Blair, 'Miss West's job will mainly consist of protecting the world from her, not her from the world. Isn't that so?'

I laughed, shaking my head. 'I want to keep my job.'

'I'll get you a glass,' said Mike. He picked up the typewriter and papers to leave the fourth chair vacant for his employer, then vanished with them into the house.

His mother glanced after him. 'I'm told we may be going to have a new play from you?'

'It may come to something. At present it's quite hideously in embryo, all beginning and no end.' He pulled one of the chairs forward and sat down between us. 'But at least it *has* a beginning. I was on the verge of deciding I'd dried for good. You know how it is? For the last few years I've been lucky, one thing so to speak begetting the next as I worked, but after *Tiger Tiger* the vein ran out.' He spread a broad hand on his knee, regarded it for a moment, then looked up at Mrs Gresham with simplicity. 'It never happened before, and it frightened me to death.'

'It was probably just the flu.' Her tone was not unsympathetic, merely matter-of-fact, and it must have touched some common chord of understanding, because he laughed, relaxing back in his chair and stretching his legs in front of him.

'Probably. If so, it wasn't such an ill wind for me after all – it blew me to Lanzarote to recuperate, and so found me this house, and my story.'

'How do you mean?'

He turned the hand, palm up. 'The story belongs here. Actually here, to this house. Something that happened here.'

'Then you've robbed me twice over,' said Mrs Gresham.

'Robbed you?'

'Certainly. That's why we're here. I'd no idea this was your house, or that my son was here. Perdita and I simply came down to look at the beach, found we couldn't go any further, and drove into your yard to turn. Thereupon I fell in love with the house and sent her along to find out who owned it, and if there was anything to be done about buying it. She ran across Michael, who was un-cooperative, and would have got rid of her in double-quick time if it hadn't turned out that I was his long-lost mother. So you see you have robbed me, first of the house, which I envy you bitterly, and now apparently of a story, too. If I had only got here first I would have fallen heir to both.'

He laughed. 'I'm very sorry.'

'Well, there's a divinity that shapes our ends. No doubt the story, whatever it is, will come off rather better as the new James Blair than as the latest adventure of Sockeye the Salmon or the Teenage Pirates. Those,' added my employer modestly, 'are two of the world-beaters I am currently engaged with. I can't expect you to know.'

'I was brought up on Beatrix Potter,' said Mr Blair, 'and if I were forty years younger I'd be an ardent fan of Sockeye the Salmon.'

'Aren't you nice? I suppose we're not allowed to know this story? I'm afraid I couldn't help seeing the title, but don't worry, silent as the grave, and of course Perdita is, too. At least tell us where it comes from? I thought the "small isles" were the Hebrides?'

'Not this time.' This from Mike, coming out of the house with a glass and another bottle. 'It's just a phrase we used translating from the Spanish.' He spoke a phrase in that language. 'That just literally means the wind from the little islands – in this case the islands off the north cape, Allegranza, Graciosa and the rest. If you've been that way you've probably seen them. James?'

'Thank you.' Mr Blair took the glass. 'Yes, I suppose the phrase "the small isles" suggested itself because it was familiar, though heaven help us, we might be on a different planet here.' He sipped the wine absently, both hands cupping the cool glass, his gaze slowly travelling over the green bubbles of cactus, the black basalt, the glittering sea, the cloudless blue, focussed seemingly not on them or beyond them but on some sharp point of light thrown by them inward into himself, as by a burning-glass. But his voice was ordinary, even faintly apologetic. 'The story . . . As a matter of fact, it's hardly a story at all, and what there is of it is so ordinary, so much the classic cliché of a love story, that told baldly like this it hardly bears repeating. But there's something there, if one could find the treatment.'

We all sat watching him. I thought to myself, there's always something there, if one can find the treatment. The same old material, the same old line, the same old setting – all that counts is the quality of the mind that processes them. And this was the man – I looked up suddenly and caught Mike Gresham watching me. His eyes flickered and he looked away quickly.

'And I can't even pretend there was anything exciting or dramatic about the way I found the material,' James Blair was saying. 'I suppose you'd gather that this used to be a small farm. It was a rather specialised kind of farm, Lanzarote style . . . As you can see, there's nothing in the way of arable, or grazing for anything except goats. It was a cochineal farm.'

'A cochineal farm?' I exclaimed.

He smiled. 'It sounds ridiculous, doesn't it? About as ridiculous as a silk-worm farm, only a cochineal farm is far less picturesque. You see those great slopes of prickly pear behind the house? That doesn't just grow there by chance, it's been deliberately planted, because it's the host to the insect from which you get cochineal. It used to be one of the main industries of Lanzarote, but with the introduction of aniline dyes the bottom dropped out of the cochineal market, and the farms which relied simply on the one product went out of business, this one among them. There's a limit to what can be done with land of this type. This has been nothing but what you might call a small run-down steading now for years, so when the last owner died the farm was put up for sale – very cheaply. The owner was the last of the family who'd lived at Playa Blanca for a couple of hundred years, and the place was sold just as it stood, furniture and all. There was nothing of any particular value, but it's real Canary Islands stuff and it suits the place and I find it attractive.'

'And then,' said Mrs Gresham, 'in the secret compartment of the old deck you found the papers?'

He laughed. 'As I said, it's all in the treatment. I did find papers, certainly, but highly unromantic ones. Simply a shelf of files, and two or three books of farm records – accounts, mostly, and on the whole not particularly interesting. Mike had a look at them – his Spanish is fairly good – but they turned out to be just a sort of log, giving details of crops, harvests, prices and so on. Well, that might have been that, except that I've never been the kind of person who could sit idly in an interesting place and not begin to think about it. It occurred to me to wonder if there were anything interesting recorded about any of the eruptions, for instance. The last big one was in 1824, and I had an idea the logs went back that far at least, so Mike and I got the books out and started hunting.'

'And you found?' I asked.

'Very little – but this in itself is interesting, wouldn't you say?'

'How?'

He turned up a hand. 'I take it you've seen the Fire Mountains in the south, and those appalling deserts and glaciers of lava? Most of it was thrown up in the eruptions of the 1730s, which went on at intervals for about six years, and devastated hundreds of square miles; then part of the same area was destroyed again in 1824. Well, there's no reference to the eruptions in the log book except to say that "Cousin Andrès from Yaiza came over with his daughter and his dromedary". He seems to have stayed, and ten years later the daughter married the son of the house. The inference one draws is that Cousin Andrès lost his house and land – and possibly the rest of his family – in the eruptions.' He looked at me. 'But it remains an inference. That's what I find interesting, humanly speaking.'

'I see. They take eruptions in their stride here.'

'Shall we say they give them rather less news-value than we give a snowstorm at home?'

'And Cousin Andrès from Yaiza gives you your story?' asked Mrs Gresham.

'No, no. A ten years' love affair is hardly dramatic material, would you say?'

'I wouldn't, certainly, but then Coralie Gray's readers like love at first sight, however much cynics like you and my son may deny it ever happens.'

'Did I?' said Mike.

'Almost certainly,' said his mother. 'It's the kind of thing young men do deny, isn't it?'

'I can see I'd better guard my real story from you with my life,' said James Blair, 'because it is love at first sight, and it would probably suit Coralie Gray down to the ground.' He hesitated. 'You'd really like to hear the rest? I'm afraid the bones are very bare as yet, but you know as well as I do, Cora, how it goes.'

I saw her smile, and knew why, but I don't think he noticed. He was moving off again into his private world. As I watched him I became conscious – as one is of a switched-on heater – of some other steadily focussing concentration. But when I glanced again at Michael, he was studying a grasshopper on the pavement beside his foot.

'After that first entry,' said James Blair, 'we read the rest of them for the time of the eruptions. Did I say that the 1824 eruptions lasted about three months? The only other reference to them was that "the wind off the small isles by God's mercy blew day and night, and carried the smoke and ash away to the south, thus sparing this end of the island."' He paused. 'That was Mike's translation. It struck me at the time. I told you the other thing that struck me – the almost routine acceptance of this kind of cataclysm. I went back through the books to see if there was the same kind of reaction, or lack of it, to local eruptions here in the north. I knew that the main eruptions at this end of the island – the ones which made the dead cinder-cones and the old lava fields that you drove through today – those eruptions would be a good deal earlier than 1824, but of course in any volcanic island there are small disturbances from time to time which may not have even been recorded, I mean at a national level. Mike and I hunted through the books to see if any of them had happened here.'

'And had they?'

'Yes, once or twice in a small way. But what caught our eyes was the same phrase again, used this time in an entry about an eruption just north of here. Is there any more wine, Mike?'

'Sure.' Mike refilled the glasses.

I said: 'If the eruption was to the north, and the "wind off the small isles" was blowing again, I suppose it would bring the gas and ashes this way?'

'Certainly it would, but, true to form, that's not what the entry was about. Something was going on here in the house on the night of the eruption that affected the writer, the farmer, a great deal more than any local volcano going off. His daughter eloped.'

'Ah,' said Cora Gresham.

'I told you this would be up your street. Her name was Maria Dolores; she was the elder daughter, and there was a fair amount of money; at that time the cochineal farm was still doing well. His name was Miguel, and he was a boy from a poor family in Mala, who used to fish from the beach down below there, the Playa Blanca. It seems nobody knew anything about it until it suddenly happened. It seems doubtful, even, if the boy and girl had exchanged more than a few words. You may be sure that at this date – it was 1879 – even if Maria Dolores didn't have an official duenna, she would be well looked after. But it

36

seems they just looked at one another and fell in love. As girls did in those days, she'd collected over the years a good dowry, clothes, household goods – you know the kind of thing – but none of it was touched; her younger sister got it all. All Dolores took with her that night was a small bundle of clothing, and her silver rosary. All the boy owned was his boat, and as far as the elopement was concerned, it was enough.'

He took a mouthful of wine. In the hot silence I could hear the small, clear ringing of a bell, as the goats strayed grazing along the cliff. From where I sat I could see three of them moving nearer in Indian file, up a path that scored a shallow diagonal across the face of the southern arm of the bay. They ambled, white and yellow-dappled, past the black gape of a crevice in the angle of the cliff, then leapt one after one over the rock beyond the retaining wall to pause, grazing apparently with relish, among the cochineal cactus.

'And that,' said James Blair, 'is all we know. She left a note for her father, but we're not told what was in it. "*Ages long ago These lovers fled away into the storm.*" Did I tell you it was St Agnes' Eve, January 20th? Only this time it wasn't the frost-wind blowing, "*pattering the sharp sleet Against the window-panes,*" it was the wind from the small isles, full of smoke and hot ash and gases. But it was, all the same, the right wind for them. They took the boat from Playa Blanca – at any rate it vanished and was never traced – and the wind would take them straight to Fuertaventura and the other islands. And in 1879, even Grand Canary was far enough away.'

'The father never tried to trace her?'

He shook his head. 'She's never mentioned again, and her younger sister fell heir to everything she should have had. Dolores is written off then and there. "Let her not return. The wind from the north still blows, and it is all she shall inherit."'

There was a short silence. Then Cora Gresham asked: 'How are you going to finish it?'

'I don't know yet. I'm still looking for the point of entry. I see it as the father's story, rather than the lovers'. I said she had been written straight off, but that wasn't strictly true. There was one other entry, made a week or so later, but not mentioning her name. It just said, "The rosary was the one I bought her in Las Palmas, of silver with each bead made like the leaf of the cochineal pear. Very pretty." Here, Mike.' He thrust his glass at Michael, and stood up abruptly. 'Now, come and see what I'm doing to your dream house, Cora.'

'Delighted to.' She got up and followed him to the edge of the patio. 'Good heavens, what's that?'

She was staring out to sea, apparently at something beyond the north arm of the bay. I stood up to see, then stared in my turn. A short way out, previously hidden from us by a jut of the cliff below, floated the ghost of a ship. Literally a ghost. It was an old fore-and-aft schooner, its warped timbers bleached to silver, which rode quietly above its grey reflection in the shelter of the curved coast. No canvas, no rope, no sign of life. A ghost ship from years ago.

'It can't be true,' I said, still staring.

'It's true enough,' said Mike from behind me. 'It's an old ship somebody in Arrecife bought a little while ago, and they've moored it down here. Weird, isn't it? It's just a shell, quite empty. I'm told the idea is to make a night club or a floating restaurant, or something of that sort. We were scared stiff they'd improve our horrible little road, and bring all the cars down this way, but there's a better track further along and they're going to use that.'

'Well, James,' said Mrs Gresham briskly, 'that's *my* story, at any rate! I take it you don't want the copyright on that? No? It's exactly what I want for my pirate story. Maybe it's not exactly the right kind of ship, but since I've never been on an old sailing ship at all, this will do marvellously. Is there any chance of getting across and looking over it?'

'I don't see why not. Mike can fix it for you, if you like. In fact we've got a boat in the bay; we can take you across ourselves, once you've got permission. Now come along, and I'll show you the house.'

As I turned to follow them Mike touched my arm. 'Will she want you to explore the ship with her and take notes, slave-girl, or could you come swimming with me?'

'Won't Mr Blair want you to row the boat, slave-boy?'

'Probably. We could leave them there and come back. Perdita—'

'Yes?'

He appeared to review, at speed, some half-dozen statements, reject them all in turn, and come back to banality with a kind of relief. 'Do you do any skin-diving?'

'Love it. Is it good here?'

'Terrific. Sandy bottom, and submerged reefs and outcrops from the cliff, and plenty of small caves where the sand runs in and there's lots of weeds and fish. Sheltered, too, so the water's usually clear. You'll come?'

'I'd love to.'

'Then let's go and put the screws on your employer,' said her son, 'and get them to make it soon, shall we?'

3

. . . Like a mermaid in sea-weed,
Pensive awhile she dreams awake . . .

KEATS: *The Eve of St Agnes*

In the event, I went without him. That evening when
Mrs Gresham mentioned the old ship in conversation with
the manager of our hotel, it turned out that the next day,
Sunday, would be the only reasonable chance she would
have of seeing over it until the following weekend. He
knew the new owner very well, he told us (a cousin of my
wife, you understand?) and he would himself telephone
immediately and seek permission. There would be no difficulty, no difficulty at all . . . Naturally, the Señora was at
liberty to go any day of the week, but she must understand
that there were men coming on Monday to assess its possibilities as a floating restaurant, and they would be coming
and going all week. So if what the Señora wanted was to
gather atmosphere, to try and visualise the ship as it had
once been . . .?

This was certainly what the Señora wanted. We set off
next morning.

Since the farm at Playa Blanca was not on the telephone,
we had not been able to warn James Blair of our prompt
return. And when for the second time our hired Volkswagen

bumped and slithered down the abominable lane the farm seemed as quiet and deserted as it had yesterday. In fact more deserted. There were no workmen there on the cliff below the cactus slope. When my knock failed to get an answer I walked right along to where the piles of sand and cement lay covered with tarpaulins against the dew. No sign of life but a family of rosy-looking bullfinches flirting and twittering over the tamarisks.

'Not a sign,' I reported to my employer. 'Sunday, of course. And the car's gone, too. What do you bet they're all at church?'

Mrs Gresham snorted. 'The day George St Bernard Shakespeare darkens the door of a church I'll eat my royalty cheque,' she said. 'Never mind, let's go down to the bay. They're probably down there swimming.'

'Their car's gone,' I repeated.

'We'll go down anyway.' She got out of the car with decision. 'There's no point in staying here. The only thing I'm afraid of is that they'll have taken the boat away and gone fishing.'

For myself, I rather hoped they had. I had horrible visions of having to row my employer out myself to the schooner. But I said nothing, just picked up my swimming things and the picnic basket and followed her down the path.

They weren't in the bay, but apart from that, luck was in for both of us. The boat – a boat – was there, and beside it at the water's edge a boy, a young man of about seventeen, stood with bare feet in the creaming shallows doing something to a fishing line.

He spoke a little English, and he and Mrs Gresham very soon came to terms. He would certainly row her out to the schooner, he said, and she could stay there as long as she liked. He would be within reach, fishing. She had only to call him, and he would come and bring her back. And the Señorita . . .?

My employer looked at me. 'Do you want to come?'

'Do I have a choice?'

'It's your day off, Sunday, remember?'

'So it is. Well, do you need me to take notes or anything, or would you feel better with someone else there?'

'No to both. All right, my dear, enjoy yourself. And don't start watching the path yet. Church doesn't come out for at least an hour.'

The boat was afloat and half out through the white breakers, before I could think of anything to say.

The water was cool, and alive with chill, stinging bubbles. I sat on a flat rock and put on my mask and flippers. The sea was tranquil, its long, shallow swells lifting and falling softly like a sleeper breathing, but since I was alone and didn't know the shore I had no intention of diving, but decided to cruise along the reefs at the surface or just below it. I adjusted my mask, gripped the mouthpiece of the snorkel in my teeth, and lowered myself into the water.

Anyone who has ever done skin-diving will tell you that there is one moment they will never forget – the first time they ever put on the mask and looked down at the bed of the sea. It is, literally, like opening a gate on a new world. And for myself the first few moments of every dive bring the rapture of discovery over again.

And this was new country. The colours and shapes, the life and tempo of this ocean bed were as different from the sea-beds I knew in the North Sea and the Mediterranean, as the Mountains of Fire were different from the Cotswold Hills.

I saw no sea-anemones, no starfish or urchins or grey

coralweed, none of the thick bladdery straps or green sea-mosses of our home water, just the clean sand, unrippled, the sharply shaped rocks, and the drifting patterns of the thin clear weed. Weeds in sable and silver and olive moved like windblown hair, like cloud, like waves themselves across a sea-bed of every shade from gold to grey and white, with the ripples of shadow and reflection pulsing across it as the sea moved. A school of tiny white fish drifted below me, a score of them all moving together like tiny paper fish on some mobile stirred by a current of air. Then all at once, twitched by some invisible master-thread, they slipped to the right and were gone. A pair of striped fish nosed across at right angles, then hung motionless a foot above their own shadows. Something emerald-green and vivid shuttled ahead of me, from shadow to light to shadow again.

I surfaced, and reached with my feet for the sandy bottom. I was not much more than breast deep. I must have been cruising with the drift of some current, for I found that I had swum – as one always does – further than I had imagined. I had gone right along one arm of the bay, and was standing now almost below the southern headland. I couldn't see the farmhouse, set back as it was from the centre of the bay's crescent, but the tops of the palm-trees were visible above the ruined outbuildings. Beyond the other arm of the bay the bleached hulk brooded over its glimmering reflection. Though I could see no sign of life aboard her my employer must be there still, as the fishing boat was a little way beyond the ship, the boy busy in the stern over net or line.

I looked up at the towering black basalt above me. The skirts of the cliff thrust out into the sea in ridges or folds, as the lava had spilled, almost like stiff pleats of black

43

velvet, forming a series of narrow coves or inlets. In cruising along the base of the cliff I had found myself passing from light to dark and back to light again, as these buttresses threw and then withdrew their shade. A little way out to sea the water whitened round black stacks of rock, some of them massive enough to act as breakwaters, so that the water along the foot of the cliff was calm.

I turned, and began to trudge back the way I had come.

I idled along the surface, the sun warm on my skin through the milky water. There was no sound but the *hush* of the far waves, and the occasional booming echo of the swell as some tongue licked into the caves and smoothed creaming under the hollow rocks. Spray hissed and whispered, and my whole body and mind were brimful of that happiness and well-being which sunlight and salt water and peace can bring.

I don't know whether it was the same emerald fish I had seen before, or one like him, but this time I came full on him at a distance of about two feet as I rounded one of the lava buttresses into a pool where the sunlight struck full on the golden floor of the sea. It was hard to say which was the more startled, the fish or I. We both stopped short, back-pedalling, staring at one another, I with delight, and the fish with no expression that I could read; there was almost certainly no delight, but there was no fear, either. He hung there just ahead of me, green and gold and kingfisher-blue in the clear water, for a full ten seconds before he jack-knifed away into the shadow of the cliff.

To this day I can't be sure if it was just reflection from the brilliant sea-bed, or if he really did switch his lights on as he went into the darkness, but I saw him flash away under the buttress, trailing light like tracer fire. I moved in to get a closer look, swimming down from the sunlit pool into the black inkwell of shadow under the cliff. For half a minute or so I had him still – a moving glimmer of green in water black as squid's ink, then I lost him. As I trod water, searching, my feet found sand and I surfaced once more, to find that I had swum right in under the cliff, and was standing at the back of a shallow cave, looking out under a low arch at the bright distant prospect of the other side of the bay.

The water came up to my armpits, and the roof of the cave was barely two feet above my head. The air was warm enough, but it smelt oozy, and in contrast to the brilliant light outside the place was gloomy and full of echoing gaps of blackness and the horrible sense of the impending weight of the cliff above. I don't like caves. Besides, the outer arch of this one barely cleared the surface of the water, and would be filled by any kind of swell. I preferred to look at the sea-bed, where motes of sunlight dropped towards me through the bright ellipse. I put my head down and pushed off in a shallow dive towards the light and the open air.

Or rather, flexed my knees to push off. I was barely afloat when something, some enormous disturbance of the water, surging into that cave like blast, drove me back off my feet and clean off balance and pitched me with a shock-wave of noise and violence and bellowing water, right up against the roof of the cave.

I must have been knocked unconscious for a few seconds. All I remember is the sudden shock, turmoil, and then blackness. My head must have struck the roof of the cave, but the mask and snorkel had taken the worst of the blow, and though I later found bruising and grazes on my back and shoulders, the chill of the water had deadened the skin, and now I felt no pain. With the breaking of the tube of course my mask had filled with water, and I suppose that, half-conscious as I was, all my instinct and sense were concentrated on the struggle to get out of the mask and into the air before I drowned. The same instinct kept me afloat, but here without any effort of mine the sea helped me. When at length I tore my mask off, gulping for air, I found I was high and dry on what seemed to be a narrow shelf of sand and shingle running steeply up against slimed and pitted rock.

I say 'seemed to be'. Because now I could see nothing. I clung to the rock, feeling the tug and suck of the sea and the pebbles which grated away from under me, pushed the soaking hair back out of my eyes and, gasping and retching for breath, tried to fight off the feeling of un-believing nightmare. The cave-mouth had disappeared. Where there had been a slit of brilliance doubled by its reflection, there was now nothing but pitch-black night and storming water and this appalling, booming echo that slammed through and through my brain and body as though I were some blind polyp lodged helpless in the roaring spiral of a shell.

But even when the tossing of the sea had smoothed a little and the echoes begun to abate, and sense came back and with it balance, the steadying of my world brought me no comfort. I realised now what had happened. A section of the cliff had slipped from above, and falling into the shallows, had set up the shock-wave that had mercifully thrown me back on to the dry inner shore of the cave. But at the same time it had sealed me in. Of the cave-mouth, the light, the outer world, there was no sign.

4

In sort of wakeful swoon, perplex'd she lay . . .
Blinded alike from sunshine and from rain.

KEATS: *The Eve of St Agnes*

It is impossible to describe the confusion of the next few
minutes, or even to remember how long I crouched,
bewildered and terrified, sightlessly clinging to my rock,
while the water swung and dragged at me, and with its
movement the trapped air under the shallow roof beat
like blast against the eardrums.

But at length the tumult subsided. The water sank to an
intermittent swell and heaving, and the terrible noise no
longer rocked the air. My throat and eyes burned with salt,
and I felt limp from the hammering I had received, but at
last I was able to loose my panic hold of the rock, and think.

I had almost written 'look about me for a way out'. This,
in fact, was what I found myself doing, eyes wide on the
dead darkness, staring from side to side as if the very
concentration of my looking could conjure up some glimmer
of light to show me the way. But no light showed. The
darkness was complete.

I do not want to remember, much less describe, the
waves of panic that beat at me periodically during all this
time, much as the sea was beating. I think the worst of it

47

was not being able to see. I knew there was air to breathe, and even the trapped air under the shallow roof felt fresh, as if there were an outlet somewhere, but claustrophobia is beyond reason, and though I told myself that Cora Gresham and the fisherman knew where I had gone, and must have seen the fall of rock, I could not sit still with the dark closing round me, and wait for them to start searching; I had to find a way out.

The first thing would obviously be to reconnoitre the mouth of the cave, but of course I now had no idea in which direction this lay. The only guess I could make was that the inrushing swell would have washed me towards the back of the cave where, in the brief glimpse I had had before the extinguisher dropped, I thought I had seen a steep narrow beach which could be the one where I now sat. I convinced myself that if I slithered straight into the water at right angles to the rock, and swam carefully forward, I should be swimming towards the new fall of stone across the cave-mouth. It was even possible, I told myself, that if some big block of the cliff, breaking off cleanly, had fallen down across the opening, there might be space underneath it through which a diver could go; and there might, as the turbulence cleared, be some glimmer of light which could be seen under water to show me the way.

The snorkel had disappeared, but I still had my mask, and this seemed to be undamaged. I put it on, lowered myself into the water and, with my hands out in front of me to protect my head, swam slowly forward.

It is not a pleasant experience, diving in darkness, when one may be diving against rock. And rock was all I found. It was not far down to the bottom, and I kept myself down there as long as I could, and as still as I could, straining my eyes through the glass in every direction. Once, some moving creature brushed my bare arm, and I had to exert every scrap of self-control I had not to gasp myself full of water, and jack-knife to the surface or up against whatever rock overhung me. It was only my emerald fish, I told myself – only the fish; and I held myself down, groping along the sand, the rock, staring blindly round me into blackness.

The trivial incident was enough, in these circumstances, to shake me badly. The moment I had convinced myself that there was nothing to be seen, no possible safe way out, I surfaced, about-turned, and floated myself cautiously back towards my beach.

And even the simple right-about-turn proved to be impossible. I miscalculated. Where my outstretched hand should have met sand and shingle, it met rock, and at the same moment my knee jarred and grounded on a subterranean ledge, and some belated swell washed me once again hard against the wall of the cave.

Luckily here the wall was as smooth as licked toffee, but the shock and unexpectedness of it threw me off balance, so that, forgetting the dangerous lowness of the roof, I grabbed for the nearest bit of wall, found a hand-hold, and heaved myself out of the water to kneel upright on the ledge.

And stayed upright, safely anchored to the slippery rock. There was plenty of headroom here. I don't know how many seconds it took me to grasp the fact that my hand-hold was a smooth metal ring embedded in the rock.

I explored it with my fingers. It was big and heavy, and obviously corroded with age. It was like one of those enormous handles you find on cathedral doors, or the rings to which you moor a boat. And you don't moor a boat – I thought, with sudden excitement – anywhere where you can't step out of it . . . Whoever had driven that ring into the rock must have stepped out on the ledge where I now knelt. This was flat and smooth, with a right-angled rise behind it just like a step . . .

It was a step, just above water level, hewn out of rock – as my questing fingers told me – but smooth and flat, and lifting in its turn to another rise, and another step . . .

I suppose if I had stopped to think it would have occurred to me that this might merely be a landing stage for boats using the cave in some long-past time for storage or shelter, but I wasn't reasoning. To the blind creature that I was, crawling about the bottom of the black well, steps led upwards, steps led somewhere out of the trap, into air and light . . .

I stripped my mask off, then, with my right hand clamped tightly on the ring, and my left arm bent above me to protect my head, slowly let myself stand upright. There was room. Above my head my hand met nothing. I straightened the arm, stretched it – nothing. I felt carefully forward with a foot. Another step . . . and another . . .

I let go the anchoring ring, and carefully, using hands and feet, began to edge my way up the steps. Four, five, six . . . and my left hand met rock, and the stairs shrank V-shaped as the staircase bent right-handed. I clambered on, all the time protecting my head.

I did not stop to wonder where the steps could possibly be going, or what purpose they could ever have served; I just blindly dragged myself up this miraculous escape from darkness towards the upper air.

And the air was fresher here. There was even a slight warmth, a reminder of sunlight not too far away.

And at last, light.

Not so much light as a faint slackening of the darkness, the promise of a gleam round some upper curve of the stairway; but it had all the collision and glory of the first light on the first day of creation. You would have thought it was a floodlight shining right down the stairs and illuminating every step. I straightened my body, dropped my hands, and ran up towards the glimmer as if the rough steps were a well-lit staircase at home, and at the top was a landing and a lighted door.

There was indeed a landing, of a sort. The steps gave on what seemed to be another cave, and the light was here, filtering somehow indirectly but effectively enough through cracks in the roof and right-hand wall – the wall which should be the outer shell of the cliff. Because the rock was black basalt it drowned, instead of reflecting, the light, but at least I could grope forward without flinching, and where there were small cracks open to the light, there might be bigger ones.

The wall to my left – immediately beside me as I emerged from the stairway – showed lighter than the rest; it even had some faint colour about it, a sort of ghost of burnt umber; and as I put a hand to it to feel my way forward I felt a different texture, crumbly, ash rather than basalt. As my hand patted and groped along it trickles of dampish ash dislodged and fell with a whisper. Behind me, like an echo, came another whisper, another fall. I stood still, my heart hammering. I was remembering what Mike had told me about the cracks in the lava crust on this side of the bay, and how the later eruptions had filled them with ash. There had been ash on the steps, I remembered; and in the swirling pool below I had been bombarded with gritty particles too heavy for sand. There must have been a fall of ash into the sea when the rock came down. Surely I hadn't climbed this miraculous stairway of escape just to find myself at the source of the avalanche?

Another fistful of the russet ash broke away just beside me, smoking down to spatter over my ankles. I moved cautiously clear, trying not to cough, and bent to smooth the sharp stuff from my bare feet. Something caught my eye, something that the fall had uncovered, a pale-coloured object lodged in the hollow the falling ash had left. It was greyish-white, and the light caught it clearly. A hand, stiffly protruding from the wall. A hand and arm, draped in a grey fold of cloth from which the ash still scaled with a pattering like small sleet.

Even the darkness had been better than this. I seem to remember standing there for quite a long time with my eyes shut, telling myself first of all that my senses had lied, that this could not possibly be a hand, and at the same time insisting – shouting to myself – that the hand was dead, and that dead hands and dead bodies do no harm . . .

I would have to look at it. Presumably when I got out of this prison (my brain shied from the word *tomb*) I would have to tell someone about it. I opened my eyes, and looked again.

It was still there, and still unmistakably a hand, but now almost immediately something about its colour and the disposal of the drapery along it brought a doubt, and with the doubt, relief.

The arm, now exposed to some way above the elbow by the constant steady crumbling of ash, was curved as if holding some large object, and from this graceful and protective-seeming curve the drapery fell in folds like the cloak of a statue. That this was what it must be I now saw. The greyish-white colour, the stony texture of flesh and drapery alike . . . It was, after all, only a statue.

Only? Under the circumstances I wasn't prepared to get excited about the possibilities of a 'discovery' – but I had to be sure. I reached forward and touched the cloak. My relieved guess had been right . . . It was stone or plaster. I left it and turned again to my quest for a way out.

It has taken a long time to tell this, but from my first moment of startled fear to the moment when I touched the arm and turned away, not more than three or four minutes can have gone by. All the time I had been conscious of the continual crumbling and falling and pattering of the ash near me. Now before I had taken three steps there was a soft, swishing rush and thud, and another section broke from the wall and mushroomed softly up from the floor at my feet.

With it fell something that went with a small dry rattle. I caught a glimpse of some white, stick-like object. A fragment – perhaps a finger? – had broken from the stone hand. The thing was probably rotten with time and damp and stress . . . it was probably slipping, and the mass of compressed ash with it . . .

I fled to the other side of the cave, feeling my way along the rough and mercifully solid basalt, with a wary eye on the rotten wall of ash. Half the statue was exposed now. It was life-sized, the arm curved to cradle something, the shoulder forward, the head bent . . . And it was certainly moving. It wavered and stirred in the now rapidly growing light.

Two seconds later, perhaps, it got through to me that it wasn't the statue that was moving; it was the light. That whatever natural light had led me up to this level had been supplemented for the last half minute by the light of a torch, held in a living hand. And that the owner of the hand was now picking his careful way down from some-where above and ahead of me, the torchlight welling in front of him through the confines of the cave.

5

And listen'd to her breathing . . .
Which when he heard, that minute did he bless,
And breathed himself.

KEATS: *The Eve of St Agnes*

It had to be Mike, of course.

Not only had it occurred to me that I must have climbed some way towards the inner curve of the bay and the environs of the farm, which was the only building hereabouts, and which must have at some time been connected with the steps and the landing stage, but also, somehow, his coming was inevitable. After the first jump and jerk of my heart when I saw the moving light, I simply stood there and waited for him. I suppose I had been knocked half silly, and then badly frightened, and so was for the time being as entirely self-centred as anyone can be; at any rate I assumed, absurdly enough, that he was coming to look for me, sent (miraculously, I suppose, for there had been no time) by his mother. I leaned against the wall and waited for him quietly, all fear stilled.

What I didn't reckon on was the fright I would give him. The sound he made was something between a gasp and a yelp, then his breath went in more smoothly and he said with commendable mildness, 'Good gracious me.'

I took a step. I was surprised to find how weak my knees felt. 'Mike. Oh – *Mike*!'

'Perdita! For heaven's sake! How in the world did you get down here?'

'I – I didn't get down. I came up. You – you did come *down*? There really is a way out up there?'

'Yes, of course I came down. We'd just got back to the house when the fall took place, and—' I heard his breath catch again as it got through to him what I had been saying. 'You said you came *up*?' The torch raked me. He said sharply: 'You were swimming? . . . You mean you came up *from the sea*? What's happened? Surely that was Mother I saw on the old ship?'

'Yes. A fisherman took her over. I didn't go with her. I was swimming, and I was in a cave down there, about halfway along the side of the bay, and there was a fall outside, and I was shut in. I – I found some steps, and started to climb—'

I broke off. Suddenly reaction and cold, together, got through to me and I began to shiver uncontrollably. 'I – I'm sorry. I got a bit of a knock when the backwash hit the cave, and then it was pitch dark and I thought I wasn't going to be able to get out—'

He took two quick steps and pulled me into his arms and held me tightly. 'Here, love, pack it in, you're all right now. We'll be out of here in two shakes.'

'Sh – shakes is the word . . . I'm sorry. I'm all right really . . . Oh, Mike, you're sure we can get out?'

'Of course we can. It's not far. Do you realise you're just about under our cactus field?' He talked on, holding me close, deliberately soothing. Warmth seemed to come out of him in waves. 'I told you we'd just got back, James and I . . . we'd been to Teguise to watch some Sunday procession he wanted to see . . . and we heard the landslip. We knew you were here, of course – saw your car in the yard – but then I saw Mother over on the schooner, and the boat just rowing back to it, so I assumed you were there, too. And the ship was obviously OK, but . . .' He paused for a moment. 'Well . . . I noticed that the slip had opened up that crevice under the cactus – you saw the one? I wanted to see how safe it was, so I came down by the goat path. I . . . I happened to have brought a torch, so when I found a lava tunnel had been opened up, that someone seemed to have used some time back . . . Well, it looked solid enough, so I went in to have a look at it.'

'But to come right down!'

He said quickly: 'I heard something moving about, and I thought one of the goats might have wandered in and got caught.'

'A goat? But Mike, you might have been trapped yourself! It could have been—'

'Yes, but it wasn't. Now we'd better get back up as quickly as we can, if you're better?'

'Yes, thanks. Sorry, I was just cold.'

'Good grief, so you are, you're frozen, and no wonder. You'd better have my jacket – here, hold the torch.'

He pushed it into my hand while he took off his jacket. 'There, put that on. Bare feet, too? You poor kid, this lava rock's damned sharp – yes, I thought so, your feet are bleeding.'

'I don't feel them. No, honestly I don't, they're too cold. Leave it, Mike, we'd better hurry. Some of the ash was slipping over there—'

But he had already kicked off his shoes, and was pulling his socks off. 'Never mind that, put these on or you'll tear your feet to pieces climbing out. My shoes are no good to you, but the socks'll help. Here.' He pushed them into my hands, and started putting his shoes back on. 'I'll take the torch now – good God!' He had caught sight of what showed in the moving beam. 'For pity's sake, what's that?'

'It's a statue,' I said. 'I saw it when the ash began to scale away.'

'Good Lord, so it is.' The beam seemed to focus and intensify as he approached the thing. He sounded pleased and mildly excited. 'Do you suppose we've discovered something valuable? How in the world did anything like that get here?'

'Maybe this was used as a storeroom. Or to hide things away during the war, or something.' I was struggling to get the second sock on, brushing the damp, sharp grit from my foot. 'That would mean it was valuable, I suppose.'

'You wouldn't store works of art in caverns on a volcanic island, one would think,' he said. 'Hm, very odd. What sort of stone, I wonder?'

'Mike, watch it, I wouldn't touch, that ash is falling all the time.' I dragged the sock on, and stood up. 'The thing's falling to bits anyway. Let's get out of here, shall we? Look, a piece fell off, we can take that with us and show anyone who's interested, and they can jolly well come themselves and prod round in this horrible cave.' I snatched up the fallen fragment of white. 'This is it, I think it's a finger—'

I stopped dead. The torchlight flicked from the wall to my face, and then down to my hand. I didn't need the light to show me what I held. It was the small bone of a human finger.

I dropped it. In the same moment, as if the downward flick of white had been a hand on the plunger, the wall came down. This time it was a big fall. It came rushing down towards us in a swishing, choking avalanche. In the flying seconds before the torch was knocked from Mike's hand and extinguished I saw the rest of the grey stone-like figure show momentarily, like a ghost against darkness. It was not one figure, but two. In the curve of that shielding arm some smaller body was huddled. I saw merely the double hump of two heads, one bent over the other, the curve of the protecting shoulder, the hand, grey and stony, ending in the delicate, brittle bones – then Mike had whirled with his back to the fall, and dragged me under him with my head pulled down against his chest, and his body arched over mine to keep off the falling ash. The torch went out.

It seemed ages before either of us dared to move. We huddled, clinging together, half buried, half choked by the clogging, shifting ash. Fortunately this was dampish, or we might have been choked in earnest; as it was, the stuff weighed heavily, shifting and pressing closer with every movement, scoring the skin and tearing like a sandstorm at the membranes of mouth and throat as one tried to breathe.

Crouching, my mouth and nose buried in Mike's shirt just above his suddenly thumping heart, I heard, with infinite relief, his little choking sneeze, and felt the cautious movement of head and shoulder above me.

'Perdita?' A hoarse whisper right at my ear.

I licked my lips. 'I'm all right. You?'

'Still alive.' He cleared his throat. 'God, that's better. It's stopped, I'm pretty sure. Hold still a minute, love, till we see what's what . . . I don't want to start this lot moving again by trying to get out too quickly. It won't be difficult, don't worry.'

'Can you see? Has it blocked the way out?'

'No, it's blocked the way you came up, as far as I can make out. Yes, I can see a little . . . I'm afraid the torch has gone, but there's enough light to get out by . . . Can you get your hands over your mouth and eyes? I don't want this stuff pouring in when I lift away from you.'

'Yes.' My hands had been spread against his chest, clinging there. I moved them cautiously in, cupping them against my face. The grit was horrible, and hurt, but I could breathe.

'Right?' His heart had slowed almost to normal now. His voice was comfortingly ordinary.

'Right.'

'Hang on then, I'll try it out.'

It was not as easy as he had made out. We were fairly tightly entangled together inside our cocoon of ash, which had engulfed us to the shoulder-blades: or rather, it had engulfed Mike, who hung over me, his body covering mine as a bird covers its young. Slowly, and with great caution, he began to lift himself off me, pushing the weight of the ash back with his shoulders a little at a time, then waiting for the displaced ash to pour into the gap before he moved again. It was, I imagine, like pulling oneself out of a quicksand, with the added difficulty that he dared not make any sudden or strong movement for fear of starting another perilous slip, or of course of engulfing me. But at last he managed to shoe-horn himself free of the ash, then, kneeling, reached his arms round me from behind, and with infinite caution began to pull me out.

It was the same crushingly slow process. With every movement the ash shifted and poured into the gaps, gripping with its abrasive weight. But I came slowly free, to the waist, to the hips, to the knees – and then with a run that sent Mike staggering backwards, still holding me, so that the pair of us rolled together clear across the floor to collapse in a hard-breathing tangle against the outer wall.

The fact that neither of us made any move to free ourselves this time was – naturally – only because we were exhausted . . . And – naturally – when I turned back into his arms I put my own round him and pulled him to me tightly. His heart had started to thud again, and this time it showed no signs of slowing down. Naturally not . . .

He said, 'We must be crazy.' Then, 'Are you warm enough now?' And later, 'You taste of salt and ashes. Lot's wife or something.'

'At least make it Eurydice.'

'And still in the underworld, my poor darling.' He let me go. 'For goodness' sake, we'd better get out of here! I don't know what we were thinking about!'

'No?'

'Oh, well . . .' he said, and gave me a hand up into the upper passageway.

At the top of the rough tunnel the sunlight waited beyond the crack in the cliff face. Mike put an arm round me and half lifted me through into the golden day.

For a minute or two I could only stand there, dazzled by the light, holding on to him and taking in great gulps of the clear beautiful air.

He shaded his eyes, looking down.

'There's Mother, look, just getting out of the boat. He's beached it. She must have been half out of her mind. They'll have been rowing along the foot of the cliff to see if they could see a sign of you.'

He let out a yell, and waved. Mrs Gresham looked up, and saw us above her on the cliff. Even at that distance, I thought I could detect a wild relief in her gestures as she waved back.

'It's a mercy she can't see what you look like, she'd go straight into orbit,' remarked Mike.

'My lover,' I said warmly. 'Though come to think of it, I must look at least as awful as you, which is saying a lot.'

He laughed. 'Making love in the dark has its points, wouldn't you say? My poor darling, do those scratches hurt?'

'Now you come to mention it, they're stinging like mad. I feel as if I'd been through several beds of nettles.'

'They'll sting worse when you get under the shower. Let's go and do that very thing, shall we? Look, Mother's got your clothes, she'll bring them up. I suppose I'll have to let you have the shower first, but I warn you, if you take more than five minutes I shall come in.'

'Make it six, I've got to wash my hair. Mike—'

'Yes?'

'I haven't said thank you for . . . looking after me the way you did.'

'Nonsense, you'd have got out all right by yourself.'

'I – I might not have. I might have been stuck down there for ages, perhaps for ever. I could have been buried alive, just the same as—'

I stopped. The air rustled in some blue flowers close by my hand. A pair of goldfinches, bright as butterflies, flew wrangling sweetly into some grey shrub with yellow flowers.

Mike's eyes met mine. They were sombre. Then he laughed. 'Worse than death? Don't relax for a minute, love, that's still to come. But first, that shower. Six minutes, mind, and not one second longer.'

6

The sculptured dead.

KEATS: The Eve of St Agnes

'But it could be, quite easily!' Mrs Gresham was excited. 'What you've found is a Guanche necropolis-cave . . . Perdita, don't you remember reading about them? Yes—' this to Mike – 'the primitive Canary people, before the Spaniards came, they mummified their dead. I think it's the only place it was ever done, apart from Egypt and Peru. They used to preserve the bodies with spices and various plants and the sap of the dragon tree, then they dried them in the sun, and wrapped them in goatskins and put them into caves. Since there aren't any proper caves in Lanzarote, they'd have to use the holes in the lava.' She looked from Michael to me. 'What do you say?'

We were all in the patio. Mike and I had showered and tended our bruises and emerged in turn to meet Mrs Gresham's transports of relief and James Blair's solicitude, which latter included a command to stay and share the Sunday cold duck and salad; so we had duly relaxed with big tulip-glasses of sherry in the shade of the palms, while Mike and I told our stories.

'What do you say?'

I shook my head. 'They weren't mummies. That wasn't

goatskin, it was like plaster or – or some kind of composition. I don't understand—'

'But the finger-bone? You're sure it was a real finger-bone?'

'Quite sure.' I looked up from my glass to find Mr Blair's eyes on me. As if he had spoken, I answered him. 'But it looked like stone, and it felt like it, too. How could it have happened like that?'

'Have you ever been to Pompeii?'

'Why, yes, but—'

I saw Mike look across at him, sharply. 'So that's it? You think it's possible?'

'It's all I can think of. Listen.' He picked up a book, and glanced at me. 'Mike gave me a quick sketch of your story while you were still in the shower, so I looked this out. It's from the *Proceedings of the Society of Antiquaries of London, 1863*, and it's an account of the excavations at Pompeii, and it tells you how they made the casts of those bodies you can see in the museum.' He began to read: '"The ashes in which the bodies were buried must have fallen in a damp state, and hardened gradually by the lapse of time, and as the soft parts of the bodies decayed and shrank a hollow was formed between the bodies and the crust of soil. This formed the cavity into which the plaster was poured. In the bony parts, the space left void being very small, the coat of plaster is proportionately thin, and many portions of the extremities and crania are left exposed. So intimately did these ashes penetrate, and so thoroughly has the cast been taken that the texture of the under garments, drawers, and a sort of inner vest with sleeves is distinctly visible . . ."' He looked up. 'It goes on to say that the folds of the dresses were quite distinct and the bones of the feet protruding.' He shut the book. 'So if they were caught by the gas, and then the ashes buried them – well, compared with the two thousand years of the Pompeii corpses, ninety years is nothing.'

'And the cement I've been pouring down the lava cracks had the same effect as the plaster at Pompeii?'

'It seems so.'

There was a short silence. 'Poor children,' said Mrs Gresham, 'they didn't get far, that night. Yes, I'm with you now, James. Are you going to tell anyone?'

'I shall have to, I think. I suppose they should have Christian burial, and then we have to see that the place is safe. The lower cave is almost certainly completely shut, and the fall that nearly caught Mike and Perdita must have sealed off the lower stair.'

'When I think of it . . .' My employer drew in her breath. 'She might never have been able to drag herself out of that alone. Thank God you went down, Michael! Of all the marvellous chances! There you are, James, that's how it happens – pure chance, luck, "denial of causality"—'

'Denial of causality be damned,' said James Blair crudely. 'He told me he was going down the cliff to find Perdita, and where the hell was the torch? I said that Perdita was over in the ship, and what did he need a torch for in the middle of the afternoon? I won't tell you exactly what he said to that because it was – well, abusive, but what it boiled down to was would I kindly shut up and stop wasting time and where the sweet so-and-so was the such-and-such torch, because he thought the old lava tunnel had opened up and he had a feeling—'

'I always thought it must be a lava tunnel.' Michael spoke smoothly, and only a little more loudly than usual. 'Most interesting, geologically speaking. If you've never seen lava stalactites, James, you should go down before we close it up.'

'What's a lava tunnel?' said I.

James Blair looked from Michael to me, and back to Michael. Then he cleared his throat. 'Very well. I should hate it to be said of me that I couldn't take direction. A lava tunnel, Perdita, is a natural hollow in a flow of molten lava. The surface crust of the lava cools by its contact with the air, and the under-layer on contact with the earth, and these layers insulate the core, so that it stays molten and goes on flowing after the outer crusts have stopped. When the supply of lava eventually ceases, the molten core empties itself – in this case into the sea – leaving a kind of hollow tunnel. That side of the bay seems to have been one such flow. And then later, with cooling and weathering, the thin upper surface – the roof of your tunnel – might crack and leave fissures which could be filled by the next eruptions of gas and ashes. Did you see the Cueva De Los Verdes, Cora?'

'Yes. Just a hole in the lava field.'

'That was the roof of a lava tunnel which had fallen in. This might eventually do the same. If the farm records went back far enough we'd probably find that the cave and the tunnel became a "smugglers' way", and the steps and landing stage were made. Or perhaps there never was a record, and Miguel had found the way by chance, as Perdita did, from the sea. It doesn't seem to have occurred to Dolores' father to look for them there.'

'"The wind from the north still blows, and it is all she shall inherit,"' said Mrs Gresham. 'Poor girl. Would it be quick?'

He hesitated. 'I think we can assume it. The people in Pompeii weren't buried alive, they were killed by the gases, and from the description, that might be what happened here. The concentration of ashes and gas must vary with the lie of the land, so the farm might tend to get off lightly while the main wind overleaped it and dropped the stuff along the headland. You might say it was the wind from the north that killed our young lovers. Oh, yes, it would be quick. A few moments of intense fear, that would be all. Merciful enough.'

I thought to myself: *Not even that. I know how she felt, and she wasn't afraid. She hadn't got further than hearing the beating of his heart, so close, and yet suddenly so sure. Never even alone together before, not properly, and, yet so sure, so sure, that it didn't matter whether 'for ever' meant life's long slow span, or only the next few quiet seconds . . .*

Mrs Gresham mistook my silence. She said quickly; 'Of course we may all be quite wrong – this is probably no such thing as we're thinking. We're obsessed with James' story, so we've rather jumped to conclusions. It wasn't the lovers at all.'

'Oh, yes, it was,' I said.

'What is it, darling?' asked Michael gently. I saw his mother glance quickly at him, but she said nothing.

'This.' I unclasped my hand and held it out to him. 'I found it in your jacket pocket, when I was cleaning the ash out. It must have fallen in when we were buried there.'

'A chain?' He picked it off my palm. It was something like a necklace, only shorter, of metal, corroded and black-ened. But you could see from the scratches that it was silver, and that each bead had been made like a leaf of the cochineal pear.

Envoi

And they are gone.

KEATS: *The Eve of St Agnes*

A kestrel swept across the bay, below eye level, the sun glinting rosy on its back. The air in the patio was still and hot, but a wind had sprung up, and above us the palm-leaves shuffled and clicked like playing cards.

'So that,' said Mrs Gresham, putting down her glass, 'really is the end of the story.'

'Not quite,' said Michael, smiling at me.

His mother raised her brows, and this time she did open her mouth to say something, but James Blair shot up from his chair with a sudden exclamation that startled us all. 'No, by God! Look there!'

It was over in a moment, so quickly that none of us could swear afterwards exactly what we saw.

Near the edge of the cliff and a short way beyond the crevice, a grove of cactus plants tilted, slid and vanished. Where they had been, a black hole gaped. Then the cliff's edge slid downwards and outwards in a cloud of dust and ash, and for a moment, no more, the side of the cave-in was exposed.

Then the wind blew in and tore the ash away in a great plume of russet-grey, and hazily through this, for the fraction of a second, we saw them there, Miguel and Dolores, her head on his heart, his body covering hers as a bird covers its young. Then the white shape fell to nothing, and vanished along the north wind into the open sky.

THE LOST ONE

◆

Read on for a recently rediscovered short story by Mary Stewart that was first published in *Woman's Journal* in 1960, and is available in print here for the first time since. Set against the backdrop of the Yorkshire Moors at night, the aptly named 'The Lost One' features the same young heroine named Perdita, who brings no less amount of pluck and courage to this classic Mary Stewart tale of suspense and intrigue . . .

I

It had been a typical late August day, which meant that there had been thunder about, and great piled-up clouds that, without actually coming to rain, threatened it continually and brought darkness early. We left Newcastle after supper, and I had the sidelights on before we reached Ebchester.

It was Friday evening, and I was tired. I would sooner have started next morning, but Mother thought it would be a good idea to leave sooner, and when Mother thinks a thing is a good idea, it saves a lot of trouble if one just does it without arguing. One does it anyway, in the end, so one might as well save wear and tear.

I had at least managed to insist that I, and not Mother, would drive the car. This is another way of saving wear and tear. However tired I may be, I don't lightly risk upsetting my nervous system for life.

So we set off, that August evening, to drive to the Lake District where we proposed to spend a peaceful week touring and staying at the best hotels. This again, was Mother's idea, and, as usual, I didn't argue. My much-loved parent may be erratic and at times maddening, but she has sound ideas about creature comfort, and I was happy to go along with them. In any case she was paying for the holiday.

'We won't be so very late,' I said. 'There's very little traffic. Surprising, for a Friday evening.'

'Are you sure this is the right road, darling?'

'Of course I'm not. But you've got the map, and you told me to turn off at that pub, so I did.'

'Oh.' Silence while she studied the map again under the dashboard light. Then she said, in rather a different tone: 'Oh.'

'I knew it,' I said. 'I did wonder, at that pub, but you were so sure—'

'Well, yes, but then we're going the wrong way for the map, and I have to turn it sideways to get right left and left right, if you follow, and then I can't read the names. But if we turn off soon to the right, over a level crossing, or is it a river? And then through some village or other, it will be a shortcut back to our road again.'

I moaned. 'Now look,' I said, 'make sure of this, will you? Last time I took one of your shortcuts—'

'I know, I know. But this is definitely right. Look, there's the river. And that place that looks like a barracks . . . yes, that's Arkenside prison. That's right. That *was* the turning. Now just keep on, and we can't go wrong. And there's no need to laugh.'

'I'm sorry. But four times out of five when we're out together . . . When you had me christened, did you know how beautifully appropriate my name was going to be?'

'Perdita? It's a very pretty name. I got it from Shakespeare.'

'I know. And it means "the lost one".'

'Well, yes, but we're not lost.'

'Not yet, we're not . . . No, no, I believe you, really I do! That did look like a prison, and that was certainly a river bridge, but all the same, don't blame me if we end up halfway up Crossfell and have to sleep in the car.'

'Darling, how untrustful of you.' Having set me on her

shortcut, she let the map drift to the floor, and settled herself back in her seat. After a while she said complacently, 'There you are. I knew this was right. Look at those lights ahead. That must be it.'

'That must be what?'

'I can't remember all the names, now, can I? The village that's on the map, where we have to turn off. Yes, what did I tell you? I'm always right, aren't I?'

'Always,' I said. Oddly enough, she really believes this, however often the contrary is proved. It's something to do with Essential, rather than Actual, Truth. Or so she says.

It was really dark now, and the bleak little village showed a grim cluster of cottages under the side of the fells. Light streamed from a building that looked like the village hall, and as we went by, a swinging door let out a gust of dance-music. Then we pushed past into the dark again, and I switched on the headlights.

It seemed that, for once, Mother really had guided us aright. The big car scudded west along the road in the wake of her driving lights. We were in unfenced country now, and from the verges the sheep's eyes glowed like sudden lamps out of the dark. Below the road and to the left was the quick gleam of shallow water sliding over stones; the infant stream of the Wear running east. Beside it the gaunt iron skeleton of some long-abandoned mine showed for a moment in the light like a rusting symbol of ruin and loneliness. There was no other traffic on the road except a gaggle of badly lit bicycles that swept downhill to meet us and fled past, the riders screaming at one another like jays.

'They ought,' said Mother primly, 'to ride in single file and all have bicycle lamps.'

'Well, of course. But they could see us coming miles

away, and they're only going down to that spree in the village we passed. They were going at some speed, weren't they?'

'Remarkable.' Mother had turned to look after them as they vanished into the dark. I was surprised to hear something like wistfulness in her voice. 'You could get up to thirty, at least, on this gradient. Scorching, we used to call it.'

'I never knew you used to ride a bike.'

'I bicycled a good deal in my youth,' she said sedately, 'and a very great pleasure it was. We had the roads more or less to ourselves in those days, and one really *saw* the country, not like—'

'Hullo!' I said sharply. 'Sorry, but half a moment—'

'What is it?'

I didn't answer. The road, rising all the time, had run in a great curve round the base of the steep fells, and now reared into a sharp gradient. And unmistakably, the car was jibbing. I thought I could hear an oddly hesitant note in the engine.

'What *is* it, dear?'

'There's something wrong. Can you hear that little knocking noise? It's not outside the car. It's the engine. There . . . Notice that? I don't think – no, we're not going to make it.'

'Make what? What are you talking about?'

'Only that you may have to spend that night on Crossfell after all,' I said, as the engine died and the car came to a silent stop on a gradient of about one in three.

I got out, found a large stone which I shoved under the back wheel as insurance, then looked about me.

It was very quiet. We seemed to be halfway up the

steep winding valley. Our lights showed a slope of turf rising sharply on the right of the road. To the left was a drop to the stream and beyond that the darkness of the rolling fells. Then, when I switched the car's lights out, nothing.

'What did you do that for? Can't you get it going again?' asked Mother.

'You know as well as I do that I could as soon take someone's appendix out as locate the distributors or differentials or whatever the bits are called. In any case these cars are owner-proof. Everything's sealed up under little bits of rubber and chrome, and I'll swear the garage keeps the keys. No, I'm afraid this is your fault for not taking it in last week when I reminded you to, so now we just sit and wait till maybe – ah!'

'What do you mean "ah"?'

'There's a light. Over there. Can you see? It's probably a farm . . . Is the torch there? Thanks. Yes, look, there's a track. It's not too far away, and surely where there's a farmhouse there might be someone to help, or at any rate there'll be a telephone. Are you coming, or would you rather wait in the car?'

'Me? Alone? An old woman alone on a deserted road in the middle of the night?' Since in fact it was barely nine o'clock, I recognised this as another bit of Essential Truth. 'No, indeed, I'm coming with you. Can you leave the car here?'

'No. I'll have to get it off the road. If you'll get out, I'll see if I can run it backwards into the farm track.'

I berthed the car carefully at the entrance to the track, and locked it. At the slam of the door I heard, from the direction of the distant light, a volley of yelping barks. 'Good,' I said. 'Someone's at home. Let's go.'

With the help of the torch we set off up the track. Our steps, in the silence, sounded loud on the stones.

The dog barked again once, sharply.

Then it fell silent, and the light went out.

'There was a light there. I know I saw a light.'

'Of course there was. I saw it,' said Mother, proving it. 'How very tiresome. They must have gone to bed.'

'It's far too early,' I protested.

'On farms they always go to bed with the hens.' We reached the farmyard, and she paused, shining the torch round the silent buildings as if wondering where the henhouse was.

'It's still too early. Come on, we can but try.' I walked resolutely across the yard and knocked on the house door. The sound echoed hollowly in the darkness. No dog barked.

I tried again. Nothing. I took the torch and shone it round me. The usual backdoor clutter; a water-butt, a couple of buckets, an iron scraper, a doormat, flattened and frayed, a kennel . . .

The length of chain that lay on the concrete was bright, and there was a collar fixed to it. I bent down and felt it. It was warm.

I showed her this. 'And it's my deduction,' I said cheerfully, 'that the farmer's wife is here alone, and nervous, so she's taken the dog indoors with her. The others'll be at the dance in the village. She's either deaf, or at the front of the house. Let's go round and see if there's a light there.'

We pushed through a sagging wicket gate which gave on what had once been the front garden. Now it was neglected and overgrown, with thick ivy clouding the walls, and a damp tangle of grass underfoot. There was ivy on the house front, too. It hung like heavy, frowning brows over the blank windows. From this side the house had that queer unused look that farmhouses get, whose traffic is all in the rear. It might have been standing empty for years.

I stood on the damp grass, staring at it, daunted. If there was anyone at home they did not, apparently, welcome strangers after dark.

From away to my left I heard Mother's sharp whisper. 'Perdita! There's a french window, and it's open! Come on.'

There was indeed a french window, and it was wide open. What's more, Mother was inside it. She floated into the darkened room like a ghost. I said desperately: 'Come out, for heaven's sake! You can't do that!'

'But it wasn't locked. When I tried it—'

'You mean it was shut? It wasn't actually standing open?'

'Of course not. But it wasn't locked. I just tried the handle – oh, *botheration*!'

This is Mother's equivalent of a really strong oath. Hovering uneasily on the threshold of the window, I asked, 'What is it?'

'I think I've laddered a stocking. They leave the chairs in the silliest places. Shine the torch here, Perdita.'

'But we really can't—'

'Hurry, darling!'

I sent the light skimming round. It showed a square, rather crowded room, which seemed to be an office-cum-parlour. There were some stuffed chairs round the empty fireplace, but the lack of radio or newspapers indicated that this was rarely, if ever, used as a sitting-room. Against the wall opposite the fireplace stood an enormous desk covered with untidy piles of papers. And among the papers, a telephone.

'There you are!' This, triumphantly, from Mother.

'But we can't!'

'If they were in,' she said reasonably, 'they'd let us. It's an emergency, so why shouldn't we use it? You can leave the money and a note on the desk.'

I took a couple of tentative steps into the room. It smelt musty and a little damp. 'It seems a dreadful thing to do. And I don't believe they're out. What about the light we saw?'

'It might have come from further up the hill. A farm cottage, or something.'

'Well, then, the dog? He was here. I heard him twice. And that collar was still warm.'

'He'd slipped it and run off.'

'He hadn't slipped it. It had been unfastened.'

'All right. But darling, there's the telephone, and we've got to get help if we're to get anywhere tonight, and why you waste time arguing when the obvious thing to do is— What on earth's the matter?'

I didn't answer. I was looking over her shoulder at the door. It was opening, slowly. I went back a step, keeping the torchlight fixed on the widening gap. Mother turned quickly and gave a little gasp.

A hand came out of the dark beyond the door, a thin hand. A woman's hand. The electric light flashed on.

I switched the torch off and stood there dumbly, trying to think of something, anything, to say. Not surprisingly, nothing came. Mother retreated smartly to an armchair and into it, looking frail and elderly and completely detached from the proceedings, as the woman came slowly into the room.

She was slightly built, with a thin sallow face and dark, greying hair pulled tightly back into a bun. She had not been on her way to bed; she wore a faded print overall over her dress. Behind her was a boy of perhaps fifteen. He was like her, wiry and dark, but with a clear high colour under the fair skin.

But I didn't take in the details of their appearance just at that moment. I only noticed one thing about them, and that was that they were both frightened.

And not of us. When they saw who had broken into their home – two women, one of them elderly – you might have expected the fear in the two pairs of eyes to abate. But it didn't. They stared at us for a full half-minute of silence. While I cleared my throat and wondered just how to begin, Mother pulled her furs round her and looked the part of Fragile Old Lady with Headstrong Daughter, and left it to me.

The woman took two faltering steps into the room, the boy hesitating behind her in the open doorway. She put one hand down on the corner of the desk, and leaned on it heavily.

'What was it you were wanting?' she asked.

2

I must have made some kind of apologetic and faltering explanation, but I don't remember what I said; there was something about the woman's obvious terror, and something about the way the boy stood there in the doorway, as if the darkness was breathing on the back of his neck, that infected me with a crawling uneasiness. I was wishing that, telephone or no telephone, we were back on that lonely road in the darkness, waiting for help from a passing motorist. It was obvious that Mother and I had walked into the middle of some serious domestic trouble, and I'd have given a lot to walk straight out again. But Mother sat there with closed eyes, looking frail and remote from it all, and there at hand was the telephone and our deliverance.

'The telephone?' The woman's voice was flat and dull, as if she had hardly been listening. 'You'd like to use the telephone?'

'Yes, please. Perhaps you know the name of a garage in Nenthead that I could get hold of?'

She made a sudden movement. 'They'll be shut.' I had her attention now. Her eyes, which were large and rather prominent in the thin face, were fixed on me painfully. I saw the convulsion of the neck-muscles as she swallowed. 'I – I'll ask. If you'll wait a minute.' Her eyes swivelled towards the door. She said sharply, 'Martin, go and see.'

But before the boy could move he was pushed to one side, and a man came forward into the light of the room. Martin wouldn't have had to go far in search of him. I could have sworn he had been standing there all the time, not a yard away, in the darkness of the passage.

He was of medium height, and thickly built, and he wore a tweed jacket that hung loosely on him, and badly fitting, patched and faded breeches. He looked powerful: his hands were hard and calloused, and his face had a craggy, weather-pitted look that disagreed oddly with his pallor. His eyes were grey, the same colour as the boy's, but they were small and badly set. It was a tough face, and not a pleasant one. The woman was watching him, and the boy Martin, who had remained just inside the doorway, never took his eyes off him. It seemed apparent that here – in this man – was the storm-centre of their fear.

He stood surveying Mother and me, with one hand tucked into his belt. His first words were not alarming. 'Well, now, ladies . . . My name's Bewlay. I heard what you were saying just now to the missus. You've a car stuck down yonder on the road above the beck, and you've broke in here to use the telephone. That it?'

'I – I'm afraid that's true, Mr Bewlay,' I said. 'We shouldn't have done it, I know, but there was no answer, and we were sure we'd seen a light, so we came round to the front, and, well, the french window—' I let it go, finishing lamely, 'I'm frightfully sorry.'

He gave a smile of a sort, that showed bad teeth. 'Don't fret yourself. We'll not call the pollis this time.' He seemed to find this funny, because he laughed, the little bright grey eyes squinting sideways at Martin. Martin didn't smile, and nor did the woman. The laugh died as Bewlay added, gruffly: 'Gave my wife a fine fright, you did, ladies, and no mistake. Burglars, she says to me, Robert, burglars. Don't talk so daft, I says, funny sort of burglars they'd be, talking at the tops of their voices and kicking the chairs about. Get yersel' down, I says, and see who it is. Likely it'll just be one of your friends, come to borrow summat this late, and the back door locked. Get down and see, I says. And here it's nobbut a slip of a bonny lass and an old woman.'

I sent Mother a hasty glance. She had opened her eyes, and was regarding Robert Bewlay with dislike. Since sixty, Mother has occasionally allowed – but with protest – the word 'elderly'. 'Old' – never.

I said quickly, 'It's awfully nice of you not to be angry.'

Again that gap-toothed grin that was, somehow, so unreassuring. 'Don't mention it.' He turned to the woman and said, roughly, 'Well, what's tha waiting for? Give the ladies a cup of tea and a bite to eat while I get on the phone for them.'

'No, look,' I protested, 'you really mustn't bother, it's so late, we really don't need anything. Besides—' I stopped. I couldn't exactly add that Mother detested tea anyway and never drank it, but even if I had I doubt if Mrs Bewlay would have taken the slightest notice. She didn't even look at me. She was watching him.

He took no notice of me, either. He said, with finality, 'You'll take a cup of tea.'

As if the words had been an order, she turned and hurried from the room. Martin made a move to follow, and was held with a rough little snarl. 'Stay where y'are.'

Feeling, by now, really uncomfortable, I tried a last feeble protest. 'It's very kind of you, Mr Bewlay, but we really mustn't put you to the trouble of telephoning as well. If you'll just give me the number—'

He was already at the desk, leafing through a dog-eared directory. 'The place at Nenthead'll be shut. I'll have to get them at the house. If he's not there I'll get a chap I know from Alston way.'

'Would they come? It's a long way.'

Again that unappetising grin. 'We live in lonely parts, miss, and folk are neighbourly. He'll come, for me, where he mightn't for you. You'd best let me know what's up with your car. Just petrol, was it?'

'No.' I told him, as best I could, what the car's symptoms had been, and he merely nodded and picked up the receiver.

'Now don't you fret, we'll get it fettled. So if you and your ma will go through into the kitchen I'll see what I can do.'

'Thank you very much,' I said, and waited for Mother to precede me down the passage and into the kitchen.

It was not exactly a cosy tea-party.

The kitchen was one of those big farmhouse places with a flagged floor and an enormous old-fashioned black fireplace made cheerful with polished brass. A rag rug lay before the fire. There was a big scrubbed table, one end of which was now covered with a red-checked cloth. Here I sat with a cup of tea, anxiously served by Mrs Bewlay. Her scared expression never altered, and she hardly seemed to be listening to Mother's gentle monologue about fruit-bottling, delivered from the rocking-chair by the fire. And it was just as well that Mrs Bewlay, hovering restlessly between Mother's cup and mine with a brimming pot of over-strong tea, wasn't listening. Mother had never, as far as I knew, bottled any fruit in her life.

The boy Martin had eventually escaped into the kitchen with us. His mother poured him a mug of tea, and he was just raising it to his lips when, from somewhere above us, came the bang of a door, and a series of odd, scuffling sounds. Martin jumped, and spilt his tea. His face, which had not lost its look of strain, now went white with what looked like pure terror.

He slammed his mug down on the table. 'That's Glen! She's got out!' he said, in a high, breathless voice, and jumped for the door.

The dog must have been shut somewhere upstairs. I could hear her now coming downstairs like a rocket, landing in the passage with a scramble and a thump, her paws slipping and scrabbling on the flags as she hurled herself towards the open kitchen door. She was in the room and half across the floor before the boy had taken three steps. She flung herself at him, a thin young cur-collie with a muzzle as sharp as a vixen's and a white blaze on her chest.

Martin said breathlessly, 'Glen! Down!' then, in a rising shout, 'Here!' as the dog, dodging his grabbing hands, raced back to the door of the parlour where the farmer was shut in with the telephone. She thrust her nose against the bottom of the door, and there came the same volley of whining yelps that I had heard earlier from the road.

Martin ran forward, shouting 'Here!' and this time the dog turned to obey, just as the door opened and Bewlay came out of the parlour. He almost tripped over the dog, cursed, and kicked it across the passage. The animal whipped round, snarling, as if to launch herself at the man, but Martin's voice, really frightened now, caught her in mid-leap.

'*Down, Glen!*'

The dog dropped, then slunk, in that foxy way that collies have, back to the boy's feet.

All pretence of good nature had vanished from Bewlay's face. He slammed the parlour door shut behind him, and strode into the kitchen, scowling at the boy. 'I'll shoot that bloody dog o' yours if you can't keep her under control! How did she get out?'

'I – I don't know.'

Mother said, clearly, from the rocking-chair, 'Mr Bewlay, you are being very helpful indeed to my daughter and myself, and we are grateful to you, but I'm afraid I cannot allow you to ill-treat an animal in my presence. The dog strikes me as being very well under control, or she would undoubtedly have bitten you. Which, in itself, seems an odd circumstance. Is she not your dog?'

For a moment I thought the man was going to lose his temper with her as well. The veins in his neck seemed to swell, and the little bright eyes were dangerous. Then he gapped his mouth into a smile. 'Well, now, I'm right sorry if it's upset you, ma'am. It's Martin's dog, that one, and she and me's never seen eye to eye since the day I caught her chasing the hens and thrashed her.'

'She's never chased hens in her life!' said Martin, hotly. 'She's the best working bitch in the dale, and—'

'Martin!' This from his mother. She was standing by the fireplace, still with the teapot in her hands. Tea was spilling from the spout onto the bright rug. She didn't notice it. She looked ill.

The boy subsided. I saw colour rush over his face and fade, leaving him as pale as before. The man, who had made a move towards him, checked himself, and turned to me. He spoke civilly enough. 'There's no-one at the garridge, like I said, and I can't get an answer at the house.

But I did get the chap from Alston, and he's starting out as soon as he can. It'll be all of half an hour before he gets here, so you're very welcome to bide here in the warm till he comes.'

I looked uncertainly at Mother. Somehow the car seemed a little haven of peace after the warring tensions of the Bewlays' farm. Then Mrs Bewlay said, in her thin, faded voice, 'You're very welcome. Indeed you are. You'll have another cup of tea, won't you?'

The words held a note almost of pleading. Mother said calmly, 'Of course. Thank you very much. We'll be glad to stay.'

Mrs Bewlay poured tea for both of us with an unsteady hand. Martin, without looking at any of us, made for the door. 'I'll put Glen in the barn.'

'And you'll come straight back, do you hear?' said Bewlay sharply. 'Your mother'll be upstairs, giving me a hand, and I want you there.'

The boy never glanced his way, but went out, the dog at his heels. Bewlay stood looking after him for a moment or two, with the gleam of something I didn't like in his small bright eyes. Then he turned to me.

'You've no call to worry. The chap from Alston'll fix you up for sure, and you'll be on your way in not much more'n half an hour. Make yourselves at home, now, do. You'll excuse us, I'm sure. There's work we were in the middle of, upstairs. Come by, Emma.'

Obedient to the jerk of his head, Mrs Bewlay followed him from the room. Their footsteps went upstairs, and trod along some uncarpeted passage overhead. A door slammed.

Mother set her cup down. 'Well, well, well,' she said, with some restraint. 'Darling, what sort of a place have you got us into now?'

'Wuthering Heights, or something precious like it. There's something awfully wrong, isn't there?'

'Oh, yes, that's obvious enough. We've probably interrupted him when he was beating her, and now he's gone upstairs to finish the job.'

'No screams,' I said shortly. I wasn't joking. The place was getting me down.

Mother regarded me thoughtfully. She wasn't looking amused either, and not in the least frail. 'Why do you suppose,' she said slowly, 'that a farmer has to look up the number of the local mechanic before he rings him up? A neighbour, too. He used the word himself.'

I stared at her.

'You'd think that would be one number he'd know by heart,' she said. 'What's more, you'd think the farmer himself, if he was going to help at all, would at least offer to take a look at the car . . . I mean, nowadays it's not horses any more, is it?'

I said blankly, 'That hadn't occurred to me. Do you mean you think there is something wrong here? Really wrong, I mean. Not just a family row?'

'It looks like it, doesn't it? I don't think it can be anything to do with us. He was civil enough, though he had a perfect right to be angry, and he is being helpful. But all the same—'

She stopped. Something in her voice as it died away made my skin prickle. I saw that she was staring past me, through the open door. I turned quickly. I don't know just what I expected to see; Robert Bewlay, perhaps, with a shotgun in his hand? But there was nobody in the passage at all.

I looked back at Mother. 'What is it?'

She said, almost in a whisper, 'Those wires. Perdita,

that's the telephone wire, isn't it? In the corner above the parlour door.'

I looked where she was pointing. It was, unmistakably, the telephone cable. It was also, unmistakably, pulled from its moorings. It hung uselss, a festoon of dead wire. And since the door to the passage had been open ever since we had been in the kitchen, the telephone must have been disconnected before Robert Bewlay had come into the parlour.

Before he had 'rung up' the garage at Alston.

Mother and I stared at one another.

I put my cup down and stood up. 'That's it. We're getting out of here, now. I don't know what's going on, and I don't care, but I don't like this place and it gives me the creeps, and there's one thing certain, however long we sit here, nobody's on his way from Alston to mend the car. So there's no reason why we should stay, is there?'

'None at all,' said Mother calmly, 'and every reason why I shouldn't have to drink any more of this abominable tea.'

She pushed her cup aside with a shudder and got to her feet, pulling her furs round her. We stood for a moment, listening. There was no sound from upstairs.

I tiptoed out and along the passage to the back door. There was neither sound nor sign of Martin returning, and, as I expected, the door was not locked. I lifted the sneck silently and opened the door a few inches. Nothing. I pulled it wider. Mother was beside me. I took her arm and we slipped softly out into the darkness, shutting the door behind us.

'Wait,' I breathed.

We stood there, close together, in the shelter of the doorway, till our eyes adjusted themselves to the gloom, and the blank wall of darkness resolved itself into the looming shapes of buildings against the background of empty sky.

Then, slowly, because I dared not use the torch, we made our way across the yard, and down the track towards the road.

3

We hurried down the track without speaking, Mother because our haste was making her breathless, myself because I was very busy thinking about the recent scene in the farmhouse.

It had been unpleasant, but it had also been decidedly odd. Bewlay hadn't been hostile; on the contrary, he had been kinder than we deserved. If he and his wife had really wanted to get rid of the strangers who had intruded on some domestic trouble, or worse, they had a perfect right to blast us out of their house with threats about illegal entry. But they had asked us in, and offered us help and refreshment. Bewlay had even pretended to telephone for us.

Having, presumably, just cut the telephone wires. Which made the thing queerer than ever, and chillingly so. What he had done seemed intended not to get us out of the way, but to detain us there at the farm. And why?

I stopped dead and my hand closed on Mother's arm.

We had rounded a bend in the track and there, below us, lay the road. I hadn't dared switch on the torch yet, but I could see the road, and the car, quite clearly. The bonnet was open, and, by the light of a powerful torch, Robert Bewlay was busy investigating something inside it.

My first thought was one of pleased gratitude; the farmer was, after all, as Mother had suggested, something of a mechanic himself, and was having a look at the trouble for us. My second was that you couldn't open the bonnet except with the controls inside the car, and the car had been locked, and I hadn't given Robert Bewlay the key.

I didn't stop to investigate these thoughts, because at that moment the engine started, and was running softly. It couldn't have been heard from the farm, but somehow, sudden in the still night, it sounded peculiarly urgent.

I said quickly, under my breath, 'Stay here! Don't let him see you!' and then walked rapidly downhill towards the car.

He was still bent over the engine, listening intently. It ran sweetly. Whatever the trouble was, he had put it right. He didn't hear me till I stopped two yards away and spoke his name. Then he shot upright and swung round on me.

'What the—?'

'How very kind of you!' I said pleasantly. 'I see you've got her going yourself. What was the matter?'

He didn't answer that. He reached sideways for the torch, which had been propped inside the bonnet, and sent the light over me, then up the track behind me. 'Where's your ma?'

'She's waiting in the kitchen.' I raised my voice against the engine's purr. 'But it occurred to me that the car might be blocking the track, so I brought the keys down to see if I could shift it so that the garage man could get by. But I see,' I added blandly, 'that I can't have locked the car after all. Careless of me.'

He didn't answer. He put out a hand and pushed the bonnet shut. Then he switched off his torch and opened the car door.

Quite suddenly, I was frightened. It was as if all the things that had happened, things that till now had been merely odd and uneasy, had shaken together to form a new pattern that spelt danger. The woman's terror, the hatred in Martin's eyes, the behaviour of the dog Glen, the cut telephone wires . . . and now the car, open and running, though its keys were in my handbag. And this man, who didn't even trouble to play the game of polite make-believe any more.

I took a steadying breath. 'Look, Mr Bewlay –' my voice was taut and a shade too high – 'I don't want to seem ungrateful, and I certainly don't want to pry into things that are none of my business, but—'

'You shut your trap and keep quiet.' The words came out of the dark quite quietly, but with a sort of suppressed and breathless violence that hit me like a physical shock. I must have stood frozen for one unbelieving half-minute, while all the flimsy shibboleths that had made up my safe, polite, well-padded world, crumpled round me and blew away into the darkness. I had been taught no answer to violence. I stood like a fool with my mouth open, wondering what to say, what to do.

I had no chance to say anything. He moved.

A hand shot out, closed on my arm, and jerked me towards him. As my breath went in for the scream, something cold and sharp – an edge of metal – touched my throat. His voice said, with that quietness furring over the terrifying impact of violence, 'I told you not to make a noise. Keep your trap shut or you'll get it. Understand?'

I didn't move.

His grip tightened. He seemed to hesitate, and I knew, as if he'd spoken it aloud, that he was wondering just what to do with me. 'Are you going to be quiet?' His voice was rough, but in the very question there was a decision, or rather a withdrawal of purpose, that slackened my bones with relief. He repeated the question, and the knife-edge stirred against my skin. I managed to nod. The knife withdrew. Still holding me, he pulled the door of the car open.

'Get in.'

I think I tried to say something, but the arm that still held me tightened again, and he half dragged, half pushed me towards the car. I couldn't see anything, but somewhere in the darkness was that cold, narrow knife . . . I got into the car, and was thrust across to the near-side as he heaved himself quickly into the driver's seat beside me. He pulled the door shut, switched on the sidelights and let the car slide forward towards the road.

I said hoarsely, 'What is all this? Where are you taking me?'

'You'll see.'

He swung the car out into the road, and turned her back down the dale, the way we had come. As she gained the smooth surface he switched on the headlights. I could see no other light anywhere in the valley. I stole a quick, sidelong glance up the track towards the farm. I thought I saw movement, somewhere behind the edge of light. Then nothing.

Beside me Bewlay said shortly, 'And don't try any funny business. I've still got that knife, and it's handy.'

I noticed that he had flung a shabby grip into the back seat, on top of the three or four elegant cases without which Mother finds it impossible to travel even for a weekend.

'What could I try?' I said. 'But you might at least tell me what all this is about? If you'd needed a lift badly enough, after all, you only had to ask.'

'That's good of you, I'm sure, but not where I'm wanting to go.'

'Where's that? And why are you taking me?'

He didn't reply. He wasn't driving fast. The hill was steep, and he was treating the big car with caution. The road curled, as I remembered, through almost three parts of a circle to pass again quite close under the hill where the farm stood.

Then suddenly I saw him raise his head. His attention must have been taken abruptly off his driving, because the car swerved and then was almost savagely righted. As he cursed I heard it again, the sound that had startled him. Faint but unmistakable, it beat through the dark with that urgency of alarm that a big bell has by night. The alarm bell of Arkenside prison.

'I see,' I said.

'What d'you see?' he asked roughly.

'Why you've stolen my car. Why you cut the telephone wires. Why Martin and his mother were terrified, and the dog tried to go for you. You've escaped from Arkenside, haven't you?'

A silence. The car picked up speed, but cautiously. Deep down on our right the stream glittered at the edge of our lights. To our left the land rose steeply.

'Little Miss Clever, eh?' I could almost see the unpleasant grin exposing the discoloured teeth. 'All right. So what?'

'How did you manage to scare Martin and his mother into helping you? You don't really own that farm, do you? What did – what's happened to the farmer?'

'I didn't do naught to the farmer. He's my step-brother, see? Him and me, we've never seen eye to eye, but I reckoned if I got up to the farm he'd have to lend a hand – some clothes and a bite of food and the loan of his car . . . But the luck was out. He's in the hospital at Durham getting his appendix out, and the car's been loaned to her brother down Eastgate way. I did get some clothes and

94

the bit of cash they had by them, and then you happened
along with your ma. Not such bad luck after all, was it?'

'What were you in for?'

'Eh?'

'What were you in for?'

'Murder.'

It is a word that carries its own shock-waves. There
was a silence, which I couldn't have broken, then I caught
a sideways glance at me. '"Robbery with violence", that's
all it was to start with, but then the old chap died. Night-
watchman, he was, and it was an accident. But what does
that matter now?' He sounded no more concerned than
if he had been talking about the weather. 'Manslaughter,
they brought it in the end, so you were lucky, you see.
I'd not get away with it twice.' This was apparently a joke.
He shook with laughter, which I didn't join.

'Why push me into the car, then? Where are we going?'

'You said you were from Newcastle. I'd have knocked
you cold and left you, but I don't know Newcastle well
enough to get through the town without asking the way,
see? Another bit of luck. There's a chap I have to contact
there, down by the docks . . . It's all fixed, and besides,
they'll be looking for a man on his own, not a chap in a
posh car like this with a pretty girl.'

'I see. And when we get there, what then?'

He didn't answer. My hands were clasped so tightly that
the bones seemed to grind together.

He said, with an abrupt change of tone: 'How much
money have you got on you?'

'About ten pounds.'

'Hand it over. No, keep your hands out of that bag.
Give me the whole thing.'

For some absurd reason this irritated me, and I said

sharply: 'I will not! I'm not stupid enough to try and fight you for the money. You can take it. But I'm damned if you get all my keys and letters and things. They'd be no use to you, so don't be silly!'

I heard his breath go in as if for an explosion of temper, then instead he gave that quick rough laugh. 'All right, keep your hair on. But hand out the cash.'

I groped in my bag with fingers that were shamefully unsteady. We were still running down the long, curling hill. We must have doubled back to pass fairly close below the farm. I wondered what they were doing there. Mother would have raised the alarm, but there was surely no way they could get help in time.

'Here's the money.'

'Ta.' He took it, and pushed it into a pocket. I could hear the satisfaction in his voice. 'And you can stop twisting your head round to see if they're after us. There's nowt they can do, so bide still, will you? They've neither telephone nor car, nothing but an old bike in the barn, and if you reckon they can get help on that before we get clear to the main road . . . Not without a bloody miracle, they can't.'

The next second the brakes went on violently, the tyres tearing at the road. I was flung forward, but managed to save myself as the car rocked to a screeching halt with a smell of burnt rubber.

The road was blocked. Something white, like a bank of fog, was moving, drifting, eddying, swirling like foam in front of us. Not fog, sheep. It was a flock of sheep. There must have been fifty of them in the road. And they weren't just crossing it; they were simply on it, milling about, circling with heads held high and eyes like points of flame, and tiny, dainty, frightened feet. More were coming down the slope, pouring down the dark grassland like a thick stream of curds into the frothing pool in the road. And in and out, round and up and down the dim slopes went a weasel-slim black streak at a flowing gallop, hustling, compelling, calming, holding them in the path of the car, a living barrier as impassable as concrete.

In the stupefied moment before either of us moved, I heard again the boom of the prison bell, and above it, sweet and high and clear like the sound of the summer moors, a distant whistle. The dog flashed across our head-lights and went up the steep hill with hardly an effort. I saw the narrow head and the triangle of white throat. Glen.

Martin had worked the miracle. From a full half-mile away, where he was still running to cut us off before we left the Bewlay land, he had blocked the road.

4

Beyond the flock lay the fork in the road: the right-hand branch was Bewlay's way to freedom; from the left would come the search party from Arkenside, making, it was to be expected, straight for the farm. Bewlay, cursing wildly, seemed to have forgotten about me in a blind red rage against Martin and the dog. He thrust his head out of the window and bellowed into the darkness:

'Get the bloody things off the road or I'll drive through them! Martin! Martin! D'you hear me?'

No reply except the tolling of the bell from Arkenside, and the boy's whistle, plaintive, with a sweet upcurving note. The sheep flowed and thickened in the road. There must have been nearly a hundred now, held there by the wheeling, weaving body of the dog, and that sweet distant whistle from the dark.

Bewlay said something violent and short, and reached for the handbrake. He was going to drive into them. If he went slowly enough the bulk of them might get out of the way so that he could force a path through without damaging the car. Perhaps it was the sudden sick vision of the carnage of blood-stained fleeces and broken limbs that spurred me back to action, but I came to myself as if water had been thrown over me.

It was no use trying to turn off the ignition. Even if I could have reached past Bewlay, he had started the engine with a piece of bent wire that looked as if it might be jammed in the switch. He still seemed to be hesitating before ramming his way into the flock. Perhaps some old instinct held him back – he himself might have been brought up to farming, after all. He had his head out of the window, and he was shouting again into the darkness: 'D'you hear me, there? I'll drive straight through yon bloody yowes if you don't clear the road!'

He had forgotten all about me. I couldn't stop him going on, but I could get out, fast. I slipped quietly out of the car and fled back beyond the range of its lights. If I could find some corner of darkness in which to hide, he would surely drive on without taking time to hunt for me?

Above the road the ground reared sharply in a grassy bluff where rough rock showed through. It was too steep to scramble up, and I didn't dare run back up the open road to look for an easy place to scale the slope. I turned the other way, and plunged down the sharp descent towards the stream.

At the foot of the slope was a stretch of smooth, sheep-bitten turf, dangerous with old rabbit-holes. Then a sharp, foot-deep drop to pebbles that scrunched and slid underfoot. Then the slithering shallows of the stream.

The lights of the car, diffused back off the darkness, showed me my way. The stream was wide here, and I hesitated, but between stream and road there was no shelter, while across the shallow water, out of reach of the headlights' glow, rose the steep shadows of the fells.

I splashed across with scarcely a pause. Once, my foot slipped and I went over the knee into a hole, but I dragged myself free and stumbled up the far bank. My soaked shoes squelched and slithered on grass. I ran on.

I found myself running, unbelievably, on concrete, while ahead of me, all around me, loomed enormous angles and perpendiculars of blackness, dimly seen, like the streets of some unlighted city. Something tripped me and almost sent me sprawling. I turned blindly to my right, only to come up against a wall with a thump that nearly knocked the breath out of my body. I swung round gasping, bewildered, my hands out in front of me as if to ward off a nightmare.

For a few dazed moments I didn't understand. Suddenly, it seemed, the bare and friendly darkness of the fells had raised out of nothing a jungle of concrete and rusting iron, a ghost town as full of menace as a spring-trap. Then I saw where I was. I had run into the tangled and rotting precincts of the ruined mine. Against the sky the shapes showed only as blocks of deeper darkness; the high squared turrets, the gaping stairways where loose sheets of corrugated iron flapped and clanked in the slight breeze of evening, the skeletons of wheels, the steep angle of a metal conveyer . . .

Somewhere, high up among the dead machinery, roosting starlings stirred on the rotting beams. Something scurried in a corner. The place breathed desolation. It was alive and creaking in the dark.

I turned to run clear of it. My foot struck something that clanged away across the concrete.

Like an echo, from somewhere quite near at hand, came the muffled thud of feet and the clink of a kicked stone.

I glanced back towards the road. The sheep were still there, crowding round the car, but straggling now, as if released from the dog's control. The car itself was stationary, and its lights were out, but the scene was vividly lit, because another car was approaching from the other direction. From Arkenside. Its headlights lit up my car, showing it empty. Bewlay, at the approach of the other car, had seen the futility of trying to crash through Martin's flock, and had run, like me, for the darkness of the fells.

He blundered up out of the shallow stream and came straight towards me.

The place was like a maze. All around me loomed the massive shapes of darkness, walls, machinery, holes that gaped where doors had long since rotted off their hinges. Well, a maze was a good place to hide in, and that was all I could do now. I didn't dare shout to tell the pursuers where he was. I no longer imagined that he would murder me, but I didn't fancy being caught and used as a hostage with that knife at my throat again. All I could do was go to ground in some corner and let him go past. He would, like me, be making for the open fells.

But I would have to be quick about it.

Softly, as softly as I could in my soaked shoes, I crept into the nearest and blackest gap of darkness. It turned out to be a doorway that opened into what felt like the space of an enormous shed.

Behind me Bewlay's steps met the concrete, and seemed to stumble. I heard the singing whine of some loose wire that he must have kicked. He hesitated, took two or three uncertain steps, then stopped. His breathing was loud. He couldn't have been more than twenty yards away.

I stood still, trying not to breathe. The darkness in the shed was as thick as black velvet.

He was moving again, carefully now. He took a few paces forward, then he stopped once more. I judged that he had got himself into some sort of shelter, and was waiting for his eyes to grow accustomed to the darkness. He would neither dare to use his torch, nor stumble on through the jungle of decaying machinery in a blind attempt to reach the open moor.

I stooped and brushed my hands along the floor in front of me. Beaten earth and a few loose stones. Bent double, patting my way, I inched along close to the wall, moving as silently as a shadow. I could see a little now, a very little. At the far end of the shed I could just discern a rectangular gap that might once have been another door. And it faced the stream. Beyond it, very near, I could hear the water chattering over its shallows. If Bewlay would only move far enough away to give me a start, I could slip out that way and run back to the road to give the alarm.

I was halfway towards the door. I paused to listen for Bewlay. Nothing. But all at once the night seemed bewilderingly full of noises. The stream, rapid and shallow, men's voices from the road, the crying of the sheep as they scattered into the fells, the creak and flap and thud of the disintegrating buildings.

He must have gone silently on his way. The faint light grew clearer beyond the doorway, as if the car had been turned with its lights facing the mine. I thought I could hear, among the men's voices, Martin's, sharp and urgent. I wondered if they had seen which way Bewlay had run.

I crept softly towards the dimly seen doorway. The sound of water grew louder, as if here the stream skirted the building closely. Wondering vaguely why a door should give on to the stream, I paused as I reached it, and flattened myself to one side of it, listening, but the sound of running water was so strong that I could hear nothing else. I edged cautiously forward until I could see out.

The doorway gave on a narrow platform of rotten boards which, to the left, vanished into darkness, and to the right sloped steeply down towards the level of the stream. Beyond the platform, directly opposite the door, was some gigantic structure I couldn't identify. It reared gaunt and black, incongruously like the Big Wheel in a half-dismantled fun fair. I could see its spokes and flanges thrusting up sharply angular against the faint glow from the road where the cars stood.

Then just behind me, somewhere in the shed, something fell with a clang of metal, and rolled noisily along the floor.

I reacted without thought. He was close behind me. He was coming. I must get out.

I shot out of that doorway like a stone from a catapult, and bolted down the right-hand ramp towards the stream.

He was halfway up it, moving quietly. I couldn't have stopped myself on that slippery gradient if I'd tried, but I don't think I even tried. Before I had fully realised that he was there, I ran straight into him, and he grabbed and held me.

He hadn't known I was there. He, too, had been looking for a way past the huge shed, but where I had gone through it, he had skirted the outside, to meet me catapulting out of the dark. He was as surprised as I was, and his reactions were faster. He gave a grunt at the impact, then his hand flashed up to cover my mouth as he hauled me close and held me. I pulled away violently, twisting and kicking, but I couldn't get free, couldn't even make a sound. With one arm tight round me and the other hand, hard and calloused, against my mouth, he thrust me, futilely struggling, back up the ramp. I came up hard against what felt like a metal railing. He forced me against it until I was bent backwards over it. It bit into me, then, ever so slightly, I felt it give. Somewhere below the ramp I was conscious of depths and darkness. Behind me the skeleton machinery towered like the Big Wheel – and of course that was exactly what it was; the huge water-wheel that had powered the workings.

The bar shifted again. It would be rotten, and it would break, and Bewlay and I together would fall into that dark pit under the rotting flanges of the wheel . . .

A shout from the road, which was answered by another, nearer at hand. The pursuers must have started down towards the mine. My captor heard them; he gave a kind of snarling grunt as his grip shifted. It was plain that no hostage plan would help him here, and he certainly couldn't drag me along with him; all he could do now was run for it – but he would have to silence me first. He relaxed his grip, and I managed to tear one arm free and claw for his face with my nails, but I was off balance, and his reach was longer than mine. I saw his free arm swing back for the blow, and the faint glimmer of the heavy metal torch in his hand.

To this day I can almost believe that I felt the blow, so hideously did I live through that split second before the crushing impact on hair and bone. But it didn't fall. Even as the torch whistled down to strike, the bar under my back shifted, moved, sank – and at the same moment something seemed to hit Bewlay from behind, so that he loosed me completely and half turned, and I went flat on my back on the broken boards of the ramp.

He fell, too, half sprawled across me, but he wasn't bothering with me any more. He seemed to be struggling, fighting with some invisible enemy, trying to turn and get to his feet. He was cursing. The darkness was a confusion of curses and violent movement and a roaring in my ears like the roar of a waterfall.

Somehow I was free and on my knees, reaching shakily for the broken rail that edged the ramp. Seconds later, half stunned and wholly bewildered, I realised that the roaring that filled the night was not in my head, it was real. Alongside the platform where I clung, below it in the once empty pit of the lasher that held the great wheel, the water rushed and tossed in a torrent. There was a splintering crack, and the roar redoubled. Water poured, whitely luminous, over the high weir above the wheel. The lasher was filling up.

Dimly I realised what had happened. The bar that had sunk under my weight was the lever that had released the sluice. It had moved only a little as Bewlay had forced me against it, but the metal was brittle with rust, and the pressure must have snapped some lever or bar that held the ancient sluice-gate. An inch had been enough, and then the weight of water gathered there, pressing against the crumbling wood, had done the rest.

I heard Bewlay curse again, and the sound of a deep, animal snarl. I pulled myself to my feet, shouting, then turned to run, just as, beside me, with a tearing creak and the slap and suck of paddles, the wheel began to turn.

It was as if the whole of the darkness tilted, tipped, and creaked over into ponderous movement. The platform shook. I could see the pale haze of spray smoking up through the gaps in the planking. I backed to the shed doorway and clung there, as Bewlay, heaving himself up with some sudden effort, trod on a rotten board that gave under his weight. The sound of rending wood cracked through the roar of water and the creak and splash of the great wheel. Then Bewlay had vanished off the ramp into the whirling water of the lasher.

5

I ran back over the unsteady boards to grip and wrench, futilely, at the iron lever.

I couldn't move it. But even if I could have forced the rusty metal back into its socket, nothing could have mended the smashed sluice and stopped the water. The wheel was gathering speed as the lasher filled. Something went with a crack like gunshot, and I saw a heavy spar break away from the wheel and slam down into the water like a flail. There was a sound like a cry from below.

I abandoned the lever and ran to the edge of the platform.

I could see, against the white turmoil of the water, the gleam and smack as the great paddles heaved themselves out of it. There was no sign of Bewlay. But then I saw something clinging to the wheel itself, a dark mass, not quite inert, spreadeagled over one of the paddles.

'Hang on!' I shouted. 'Hang on! It'll carry you up!'

No response but he seemed to spread himself wider and flatter against the wheel. It was bringing him up towards the level of the platform. I could see the suck and drag of the water as his body left it, and then a silvered sheet of it pouring off him and cascading down over the edges of the paddles below him.

I realised then that the ramp was shaking to the beat

of running feet. Martin's voice, shrill and hoarse, was calling something. Then he was at my elbow, looking down.

I leaned over as far as I dared. 'Get nearer this side, can you? I can't stop the wheel! Do you hear me? *I can't stop it!* Come nearer, then we can pull you off!'

Martin gripped my arm and shook it. 'Glen? Where's Glen?'

Then I understood. It had been the dog, attacking out of the dark, that had saved me from that murderous blow of Bewlay's. He had been struggling to pull himself free of her when he had stepped back on that piece of rotten planking. And she had gone with him into the lasher.

'Glen!' cried Martin again, then, 'Oh, my God, there! Look!'

Bewlay's legs were just coming clear of the water. I saw him make a convulsive movement, as if in answer to my shout, a heave and a jerk as if he was freeing himself of some burden; a quick kick back and down, and then he was clear of the water and travelling slowly upwards.

Martin said, hoarsely, as if he didn't believe it, 'He's kicked her back in.'

It was true. The dog must have been clinging on to him as they went in together, clinging with teeth and paws to his clothes, and then to the paddle as the wheel lifted the two bodies clear. I got only a glimpse of her as she was swept back into the race. The noise of the water was stupefying. I thought for a moment that I could see another desperate scrabbling of paws against the paddle, then she vanished.

The platform shook and thudded with running feet.

Men, voices, torchlight, Martin shouting, 'Glen! This way!' on a note of panic. Someone else yelling, 'It's th'old wheel! He's on it! Get him afore it takes him down again!' And then, sharply, 'What's that girl doing?'

I don't consciously remember deciding to do anything. I remember seeing the dog's muzzle, mute and gleaming and starred with white, come up once just below me, then the thin body, shining like a porpoise, being turned over in the foam and sucked down again. I was flat on my face on the boards, reaching vainly to grab it. Behind me, now, the platform was milling with men as Bewlay was dragged off the wheel by rough, ready hands. I couldn't reach the water. Something dark surfaced just beyond my hand. A paw came up, scraped at the slippery wall and vanished into an eddy that swirled toward the wheel. I went in after it.

My first sensation was one of anticlimax. I could touch the bottom. As yet there could not have been more than five feet of water in the lasher. But this was only a momentary comfort, because the water took hold of me, and in that confusion of noise and roaring movement and terror, only instinct, fighting blind, could keep life above the surface. They told me afterwards that I was only in for half a minute. It seemed like an hour. There was an infinity of choking, tossing blackness, while I swallowed water and flailed about blindly, knocking myself against the side of the lasher and hardly knowing, against the cold and sudden fury of the water, what I was there for. Something hit me and floated away. I made a grab for it, but it was only a broken spar. I saw it whirl up against the moving wheel and smash into splintered pieces. Then something else went by me in the swirl, and I grabbed again. The dog's fur was plastered cold and slippery as a seal's, but I managed to grab a leg, and then hauled her tight against my body and held her there.

Only then did I realise that I couldn't get out of the lasher. There was no way to climb the sheer, slippery walls, and I knew I didn't have the strength to hold myself on the wheel and let it lift me. Once clear of the water, Glen and I would be dead weight, clinging to the cracking wood. Nor would I be able to stop myself being swept against the paddles, jammed and smashed against them, perhaps, like the splintered spar.

I clawed at the wall as I was dragged along it towards the wheel. My fingers slipped and scraped on slime. I couldn't even fight my way with the stream, away from the wheel; the eddy caught and dragged me back towards those crushing paddles . . .

It drove me hard against something, and held me there. My free hand grabbed, clung. It was a sheet of some metal mesh, a big rusting iron lattice, such as they sometimes use in laying roads. The men had thrust it down between me and the race under the wheel, and it took my body like a netted fish. I hung on limpet-like, one arm thrust right through the mesh, the other holding the dog tightly against me, while I tried to summon up the strength to climb it.

Then someone shouted, 'Hang on! We'll pull you up! Hold tight!' and the lattice began to move.

The rusty metal bit into my arm as the angle sharpened, but the cold stopped me from feeling pain. The water dragged and savaged at my waist, hips, thighs. Hands took hold of me, and pulled strongly. And just as I was dragged out, dripping, onto the boards, the dog squirmed in my arms and began to cough. Someone said,

'First time I ever landed a mermaid,' and someone else, who was trying to pull off my soaked and icy coat, added, with conviction, 'That was the silliest bloody thing I ever seen anyone do in my life.' And then Martin's voice, 'Glen. Oh, Glen.'

The rest is confusion. I suppose Bewlay was taken away. I didn't see him go. Somewhere, in the kindly dark, I got out of my soaked outer clothes, and was wrapped in a coat lent by one of the men, who, stolidly ignoring my feeble protests that I was quite unhurt and only slightly shaken, picked me up bodily and carried me across the stream, back towards the road. Martin set off beside us, carrying Glen, but she protested rather more strongly than I had done, and was put down, whereupon she promptly and repeatedly shook herself over everyone within reach, and then leaped and wriggled round Martin, apparently none the worse for her adventure.

There were still a few sheep in the road. The Arkenside car had gone, and Bewlay with it, but another car stood near mine. It seemed that a neighbouring farmer, Mr Walton, with a car-load of friends coming home from a day in Kendal, had stopped to help the police and the men from Arkenside. The parked cars, with their lights on, looked cheerful and homely and familiar. My rescuer, who was, as I soon discovered, Mr Walton himself, plodded towards them across the grass, and had just begun to climb the steep bank towards the road, when a sound from the hill made everyone start and turn. It was the sort of screech that is usually described as eldritch, and, coming out of the distant dark, it was something to raise the hair and turn the mind to thoughts of broomsticks and Black Sabbaths and orgies on All Hallows' E'en.

'What the hell's that?' asked someone.

I said, feebly, 'Oh, dear heaven, no!'

Mr Walton had stopped abruptly on the grass verge of the road. I was fidgeting in his arms, wanting to be put down, but he didn't seem to notice. He stood there rigid, his mouth slightly open, staring up the hill.

'It's an old girl on – my God, yes, on a bicycle!'

'Just look at that!' said Martin, awed. 'Would you credit it? She's not half travelling, is she? She must have found my old bike – it was in the barn—'

His voice changed, and he started forward. 'It's got no brakes! The cable broke, so I put it by. She doesn't know!'

'She does now,' I said grimly.

She did indeed. She came sweeping down out of the night, knocking up a smart thirty-five miles an hour, and shrieking as she came. The bicycle bell was going violently, and quite unnecessarily, as none of us would have put a foot on the road for love nor money, and Glen, the only one who wanted to, was held fast by her master.

She saw us and waved wildly, gave a ferocious wobble, and a cry that I thought was '*Achtung!*' as she swept down towards the parked cars and what remained of Martin's flock, and then, 'Sheep! Shee-ep!' and, finally and splendidly, 'Fore!' and she was among them.

And the sheep fled. What Bewlay and the big car had failed to do, Mother and her bicycle managed in three-and-a-half seconds flat. She swept past the parked cars, did a quick in-and-out between two startled ewes, gave another a quick shove on the rump with the flat of her foot, and she was through. She vanished up the next gradient into the darkness.

A man said, 'Phew!' and wiped his brow.

The remaining sheep, demoralised, bounded about in the road.

Martin began to laugh, and loosed Glen, who jumped to lick his face. 'That'll do, now,' he said sternly. 'Come on and we'll get the yowes off the road before she comes back.'

'Rum old girl,' said Mr Walton, still clutching me to him. 'Shouldn't be out loose, if you ask me.'

'I've often said so myself,' I said. 'That's my mother.'

That did it. He almost dropped me. Then Mother was with us again, this time at a decorous pace. One of the men helped her dismount and relieved her of the bicycle as she hurried to me.

'Perdita? What happened? Darling, are you all right?'

'Yes, quite. Mother—'

'You're not hurt? He didn't harm you?'

'No, darling, truly. It's quite okay.'

'All these men – and that bell's stopped. Do I gather they caught him?'

'They did. The police were here, and some men from Arkenside. This is Mr Walton, Mother, Martin's neighbour from the farm down the valley, and his friends. They stopped to give a hand, and Mr Walton was kind enough to help me.'

'So I saw,' said Mother, smiling, and held out a hand. The farmer took it, I thought gingerly, and muttered something, then the other men crowded round and I joined in with my thanks and eventually, as the rescue party began to take its leave, heading for Mr Walton's car, she came anxiously back to me.

'Darling, you're sure you're all right? When I saw you with that dreadful man – he really is safely put away again?'

'Certainly. He's back in his cell by now, I should think. And it really is okay, Mother, he never touched me, once he'd shoved me into the car. You knew about him, then? Who he was, I mean?'

'Oh, yes. When I saw you get into the car with him I ran back to the farm, and Mrs Bewlay told me what had been happening, and I was so afraid for you, but then we heard the alarm bell, and Martin said he thought he could stop the car for long enough—'

'He did, too, he and Glen. Which reminds me. Mr Walton! Don't forget your coat! If you'll just give me a minute—'

'Nay, lass, you keep that on,' said the farmer. 'I'll get it from Emma Bewlay next time I come by. And you'd best get back there now and get yourself dry, or you'll be catching your death. Good night. Good night, missus. And good work, Martin, lad.' And with warm wishes and further offers of help, should it be needed, he got into his car and drove off.

'Dry?' said Mother peering, and only then seeming to notice how I was dressed. 'What does he mean, get yourself dry? For goodness' sake, child, where on earth have you been, and what in the world have you got on?'

'Mr Walton's coat,' said Martin gruffly. 'She went in the water after Glen, and they both might have been drowned.' Then, abruptly, to me: 'You're shivering. We've got to get back. You'll have clothes in the car for a change? Well, if you and your ma can take the car up, I'll bring the bike along. And they said the police would be coming up soon to hear what happened, so I know Mum'd take it kindly if you and the old lady'd bide with her till all's done. I reckon you could do with a bite to eat?' He looked at Mother. 'And maybe take a nice cup of tea?'

'Why, Martin, thank you,' said Mother. 'There's nothing I'd like better.'

Now read on for a taste of Mary Stewart's
beloved tale of adventure and suspense.

◆

THIS ROUGH MAGIC

I

. . . A relation for a breakfast.
The Tempest. Act v. Scene 1.

'And if it's a boy,' said Phyllida cheerfully, 'we'll call him Prospero.'

I laughed. 'Poor little chap, why on earth? Oh, of course . . . Has someone been telling you that Corfu was Shakespeare's magic island for *The Tempest*?'

'As a matter of fact, yes, the other day, but for goodness' sake don't ask me about it now. Whatever you may be used to, I draw the line at Shakespeare for breakfast.' My sister yawned, stretched out a foot into the sunshine at the edge of the terrace, and admired the expensive beach sandal on it. 'I didn't mean that, anyway, I only meant that we've already got a Miranda here, and a Spiro, which may not be short for Prospero, but sounds very like it.'

'Oh? It sounds highly romantic. Who are they?'

'A local boy and girl: they're twins.'

'Good heavens. Papa must be a literary gent?'

Phyllida smiled. 'You could say so.'

Something in her expression roused my curiosity, just as something else told me she had meant to; so I –

who can be every bit as provoking as Phyllida when I try – said merely: 'Well, in that case hadn't you better have a change? How about Caliban for your unborn young? It fits like a glove.'

'Why?' she demanded indignantly.

' "This blue-eyed hag was hither brought with child," ' I quoted. 'Is there some more coffee?'

'Of course. Here. Oh, my goodness, it's nice to have you here, Lucy! I suppose I oughtn't to call it luck that you were free to come just now, but I'm awfully glad you could. This is heaven after Rome.'

'And paradise after London. I feel different already. When I think where I was this time yesterday . . . and when I *think* about the rain . . .'

I shuddered, and drank my coffee, leaning back in my chair to gaze out across pine tops furry with gold towards the sparkling sea, and surrendering myself to the dreamlike feeling that marks the start of a holiday in a place like this when one is tired, and has been transported overnight from the April chill of England to the sunlight of a magic island in the Ionian Sea.

Perhaps I should explain (for those who are not so lucky as I) that Corfu is an island off the west coast of Greece. It is long and sickle-shaped, and lies along the curve of the coast; at its nearest, in the north, it is barely two miles off the Albanian mainland, but from the town of Corfu, which is about half-way down the curve of the sickle, the coast of Greece is about seven or eight miles distant. At its northern end the island is broad and mountainous, trailing off through rich valleys and ever-decreasing hills into the long, flat scorpion's tail of the south from which some think that Corfu, or Kerkyra, gets its name.

My sister's house lies some twelve miles north of Corfu town, where the coast begins its curve towards the mainland, and where the foothills of Mount Pantokrator provide shelter for the rich little pocket of land which has been part of her husband's family property for a good many years.

My sister Phyllida is three years older than I, and when she was twenty she married a Roman banker, Leonardo Forli. His family had settled in Corfu during the Venetian occupation of that island, and had managed somehow to survive the various subsequent 'occupations' with their small estate more or less intact, and had even, like the Vicar of Bray, contrived to prosper. It was under the British Protectorate that Leo's great-grandfather had built the pretentious and romantic Castello dei Fiori in the woods above the little bay where the estate ran down to the sea. He had planted vineyards, and orange orchards, including a small plantation (if that is the word) of the Japanese miniature oranges called *koùm koyàt* for which the Forli estate later became famous. He even cleared space in the woods for a garden, and built – beyond the southern arm of the bay and just out of sight of the Castello – a jetty and a vast boat-house which (according to Phyllida) would almost have housed the Sixth Fleet, and had indeed housed the complicated flock of vessels in which his guests used to visit him. In his day, I gathered, the Castello had been the scene of one large and continuous house-party: in summer they sailed and fished, and in the fall there were hunting-parties, when thirty or so guests would invade the Greek and Albanian mainlands to harry the birds and ibexes.

But those days had vanished with the first war, and the family moved to Rome, though without selling the Castello, which remained, through the twenties and thirties, their summer home. The shifting fortunes of the Second World War almost destroyed the estate, but the Forlis emerged in post-war Rome with the family fortunes mysteriously repaired, and the then Forli Senior – Leo's father – turned his attention once more to the Corfu property. He had done something to restore the place, but after his death three years ago his son had decided that the Castello's rubbed and faded splendours were no longer for him, and had built a pair of smallish modern villas – in reality twin bungalows – on the two headlands enclosing the bay of which the Castello overlooked the centre. He and Phyllida themselves used the Villa Forli, as they called the house on the northern headland; its twin, the Villa Rotha, stood to the south of the bay above the creek where the boat-house was. The Villa Rotha had been rented by an Englishman, a Mr. Manning, who had been there since the previous autumn working on a book. ('You know the kind,' said my sister, 'all photographs, with a thin trickle of text in large type, but they're *good*.') The three houses were connected with the road by the main drive to the Castello, and with each other by various paths through the woods and down into the bay.

This year the hot spring in Rome, with worse promised, had driven the Forlis early to Corfu. Phyllida, who was pregnant, had been feeling the heat badly, so had been persuaded to leave the two older children (whose school term was still running) with their grandmother, and Leo had brought her over a few days before I arrived, but had had to go back to his business in Rome, with the promise to fly over when he could at weekends, and to bring the children for Easter. So Phyllida, hearing that I was currently at a loose end, had written begging me to join her in Corfu and keep her company.

The invitation couldn't have been better timed. The play I was in had just folded after the merest face-saver of a run, and I was out of a job. That the job had been my first in London – my 'big chance' – accounted partly for my present depression. There was nothing more on the cards: the agencies were polite, but evasive: and besides, we had had a dreadful winter and I was tired, dispirited, and seriously wondering, at twenty-five, if I had made a fool of myself in insisting against all advice on the stage as a career. But – as everyone knows who has anything to do with it – the stage is not a profession, but a virus, and I had it. So I had worked and scraped my way through the usual beginnings until last year, when I had finally decided, after three years of juvenile leads in provincial rep., that it was time to try my luck in London. And luck had seemed at last to be with me. After ten months or so of television walk-ons and the odd commercial, I had landed a promising part, only to have the play fold under me like a dying camel, after a two-months run.

But at least I could count myself luckier than the

other few thousand still fighting their way towards the bottom rung of the ladder: while they were sitting in the agents' stuffy offices here was I on the terrace of the Villa Forli, with as many weeks in front of me as I cared to take in the dazzling sunshine of Corfu.

The terrace was a wide, tiled platform perched at the end of the promontory where wooded cliffs fell steeply to the sea. Below the balustrade hung cloud on cloud of pines, already smelling warm and spicy in the morning sun. Behind the house and to either side sloped the cool woods where small birds flashed and twittered. The bay itself was hidden by trees, but the view ahead was glorious – a stretch of the calm, shimmering Gulf that lies in the curved arm of Corfu. Away northward, across the dark blue strait, loomed, insubstantial as mist, the ghostly snows of Albania.

It was a scene of the most profound and enchanted peace. No sound but the birds; nothing in sight but trees and sky and sun-reflecting sea.

I sighed. 'Well, if it isn't Prospero's magic island it ought to be . . . Who are these romantic twins of yours, anyway?'

'Spiro and Miranda? Oh, they belong to the woman who works for us here, Maria. She has that cottage at the main Castello gate – you'd see it last night on your way in from the airport.'

'I remember a light there . . . A tiny place, wasn't it? So they're Corfu people – what's the word? Corfu-sians?'

She laughed. 'Idiot. Corfiotes. Yes, they're Corfiote peasants. The brother works for Godfrey Manning over at the Villa Rotha. Miranda helps her mother here.'

'Peasants?' Mildly intrigued, I gave her the lead I thought she wanted. 'It does seem a bit odd to find those names here. Who was this well-read father of theirs, then? Leo?'

'Leo,' said his loving wife, 'has to my certain knowledge read nothing but the Roman *Financial Times* for the last eight years. He'd think "Prospero and Miranda" was the name of an Investment Trust. No, it's even odder than you think, my love . . .' She gave her small cat-and-canary smile, the one I recognised as preceding the more far-fetched flights of gossip that she calls 'interesting facts that I feel you ought to know' . . . 'Actually, Spiro's officially called after the island saint – every second boy's called Spiridion in Corfu – but since our distinguished tenant at the Castello was responsible for the christening – and for the twins as well, one gathers – I'll bet he's down as Prospero in the parish register, or whatever they have here.'

'Your "distinguished tenant"?' This was obviously the *bonne bouche* she had been saving for me, but I looked at her in some surprise, remembering the vivid description she had once given me of the Castello dei Fiori: 'tatty beyond words, sort of Wagnerian Gothic, like a set for a musical version of *Dracula*'. I wondered who could have been persuaded to pay for these operatic splendours. 'Someone's rented Valhalla, then? Aren't you lucky. Who?'

'Julian Gale.'

'*Julian Gale?*' I sat up abruptly, staring at her. 'You can't mean – *do* you mean Julian Gale? The actor?'

'As ever was.' My sister looked pleased with the effect she had produced. I was wide awake now, as I had certainly not been during the long recital of our family affairs earlier. Sir Julian Gale was not only 'an actor', he had been one of the more brilliant lights of the English theatre for more years than I could well remember. And, more recently, one of its mysteries.

'Well!' I said. 'So this is where he went.'

'I thought you'd be interested,' said Phyl, rather smugly.

'I'll say I am! Everyone's still wondering, on and off, why he packed it in like that two years ago. Of course I knew he'd been ill after that ghastly accident, but to give it up and then just quietly vanish . . . You should have heard the rumours.'

'I can imagine. We've our own brand here. But don't go all shiny-eyed and imagine you'll get anywhere near him, my child. He's here for privacy, and I mean for privacy. He doesn't go out at all – socially, that is – except to the houses of a couple of friends, and they've got *Trespassers Will Be Shot* plastered at intervals of one yard all over the grounds, and the gardener throws all callers over the cliff into the sea.'

'I shan't worry him. I think too darned much of him for that. I suppose you must have met him. How is he?'

'Oh, I – he seems all right. Just doesn't get around, that's all. I've only met him a couple of times. Actually it was he who told me that Corfu was supposed to be the setting of *The Tempest*.' She glanced at me sideways. 'I – er – I suppose you'd allow him to be "a literary gent"?'

But this time I ignored the lead. '*The Tempest* was his swan-song,' I said. 'I saw it at Stratford, the last performance, and cried my eyes out over the "this rough magic I here abjure" bit. Is that what made him choose Corfu to retire to?'

She laughed. 'I doubt it. Didn't you know he was practically a native? He was here during the war, and apparently stayed on for a bit after it was over, and then I'm told he used to bring his family back almost every year for holidays, when the children were young. They had a house near Ipsos, and kept it on till quite recently, but it was sold after his wife and daughter were killed. However, I suppose he still had . . . connections . . . here, so when he thought of retiring he remembered the Castello. We hadn't meant to let the place, it wasn't really fit, but he was so anxious to find somewhere quite isolated and quiet, and it really did seem a godsend that the Castello was empty, with Maria and her family just next door; so Leo let it go. Maria and the twins turned to and fixed up a few of the rooms, and there's a couple who live at the far side of the orange orchards; they look after the place, and their grandson does the Castello garden and helps around, so for anyone who really only wants peace and privacy I suppose it's a pretty fair bargain . . . Well, that's our little colony. I won't say it's just another St Trop. in the height of the season, but there's plenty of what you want, if it's only peace and sunshine and bathing.'

'Suits me,' I said dreamily. 'Oh, how it suits me.'

'D'you want to go down this morning?'

'I'd love to. Where?'

'Well, the bay, of course. It's down that way.' She pointed vaguely through the trees.

'I thought you said there were notices warning trespassers off?'

'Oh, goodness, not literally, and not from the beach, anyway, only the grounds. We'd never let anyone else have the bay, that's what we come here for! Actually it's quite nice straight down from here on the north side of the headland where our own little jetty is, but there's sand in the bay, and it's heaven for lying about, and quite private . . . Well, you do as you like. I might go down later, but if you want to swim this morning, I'll get Miranda to show you the way.'

'She's here now?'

'Darling,' said my sister, 'You're in the lap of vulgar luxury now, remember? Did you think I made the coffee myself?'

'Get you, Contessa,' I said, crudely. 'I can remember the day—'

I broke off as a girl came out on to the terrace with a tray, to clear away the breakfast things. She eyed me curiously, with that unabashed stare of the Greeks which one learns to get used to, as it is virtually impossible to stare it down in return, and smiled at me, the smile broadening into a grin as I tried a 'Good morning' in Greek – a phrase which was, as yet, my whole vocabulary. She was short and stockily built, with a thick neck and round face, and heavy brows almost meeting over her nose. Her bright dark eyes and warm skin were attractive with the simple, animal attraction of youth and health. The dress of faded red suited her, giving her a sort of dark, gentle glow that was very different from the electric sparkle of the urban expatriate Greeks I had met. She looked about seventeen.

My attempt to greet her undammed a flood of delighted Greek which my sister, laughing, managed at length to stem.

'She doesn't understand, Miranda, she only knows two words. Speak English. Will you show her the way down to the beach when you've cleared away, please?'

'Of course! I shall be pleased!'

She looked more than pleased, she looked so delighted that I smiled to myself, presuming cynically that it was probably only pleasure at having an outing in the middle of a working morning. As it happened, I was wrong. Coming so recently from the grey depressions of London and the backstage bad tempers of failure, I wasn't able as yet to grasp the Greek's simple delight in doing anyone a service.

She began to pile the breakfast dishes on her tray with clattering vigour. 'I shall not be long. A minute, only a minute . . .'

'And that means half an hour,' said my sister placidly, as the girl bustled out. 'Anyway, what's the hurry? You've all the time in the world.'

'So I have,' I said, in deep contentment.

The way to the beach was a shady path quilted with pine needles. It twisted through the trees, to lead out suddenly into a small clearing where a stream, trickling down to the sea, was trapped in a sunny pool under a bank of honeysuckle.

Here the path forked, one track going uphill, deeper into the woods, the other turning down steeply through pines and golden oaks towards the sea.

Miranda paused and pointed downhill. 'That is the way you go. The other is to the Castello, and it is private. Nobody goes that way, it is only to the house, you understand.'

'Whereabouts is the other villa, Mr Manning's?'

'On the other side of the bay, at the top of the cliff. You cannot see it from the beach because the trees are in the way, but there is a path going like this' – she sketched a steep zigzag – 'from the boat-house up the cliff. My brother works there, my brother Spiro. It is a fine house, very beautiful, like the Signora's, though of course not so wonderful as the Castello. *That* is like a palace.'

'So I believe. Does your father work on the estate, too?'

The query was no more than idle; I had completely forgotten Phyllida's nonsense, and hadn't believed it anyway, but to my intense embarrassment the girl hesitated, and I wondered for one horrified second if Phyllida had been right. I did not know, then, that the Greek takes the most intensely personal questions serenely for granted, just as he asks them himself, and I had begun to stammer something, but Miranda was already answering:

'Many years ago my father left us. He went over there.'

'Over there' was at the moment a wall of trees laced with shrubs of myrtle, but I knew what lay beyond them; the grim, shut land of Communist Albania.

'You mean as a prisoner?' I asked, horrified.

She shook her head. 'No. He was a Communist. We lived then in Argyrathes, in the south of Corfu, and in that part of the island there are many such.' She hesitated. 'I do not know why this is. It is different in the north, where my mother comes from.' She spoke as if the island were four hundred miles long instead of forty, but I believed her. Where two Greeks are gathered together, there will be at least three political parties represented, and possibly more.

'You've never heard from him?'

'Never. In the old days my mother still hoped, but now, of course, the frontiers are shut to all, and no one can pass in or out. If he is still alive, he must stay there. But we do not know this either.'

'D'you mean that no one can travel to Albania?'

'No one.' The black eyes suddenly glittered to life, as if something had sparked behind their placid orbs. 'Except those who break the law.'

'Not a law I'd care to break myself.' Those alien snows had looked high and cold and cruel. I said awkwardly: 'I'm sorry, Miranda. It must be an unhappy business for your mother.'

She shrugged. 'It is a long time ago. Fourteen years. I do not even know if I remember him. And we have Spiro to look after us.' The sparkle again. 'He works for Mr Manning, I told you this – with the boat, and with the car, a wonderful car, very expensive – and also with the photographs that Mr Manning is taking for a book. He has said that when the book is finished – a real book that is sold in the shops – he will put Spiro's name in it, in print. Imagine! Oh, there is nothing that Spiro cannot do! He is my twin, you understand.'

'Is he like you?'

She looked surprised. 'Like me? Why, no, he is a man, and have I not just told you that he is clever? Me, I am not clever, but then I am a woman, and there is no need. With men it is different. Yes?'

'So the men say.' I laughed. 'Well, thanks very much for showing me the way. Will you tell my sister that I'll be back in good time for lunch?'

I turned down the steep path under the pines. As I reached the first bend something made me glance back towards the clearing.

Miranda had gone. But I thought I saw a whisk of faded scarlet, not from the direction of the Villa Forli, but higher up in the woods, on the forbidden path to the Castello.

2

Sir, I am vex'd.

IV. 1.

THE bay was small and sheltered, a sickle of pure white
sand holding back the aquamarine sea, and held in its
turn by the towering backdrop of cliff and pine and
golden-green trees. My path led me steeply down past
a knot of young oaks, straight on to the sand. I changed
quickly in a sheltered corner, and walked out into the
white blaze of the sun.

The bay was deserted and very quiet. To either side
of it the wooded promontories thrust out into the calm,
glittering water. Beyond them the sea deepened
through peacock shades to a rich, dark blue, where
the mountains of Epirus floated in the clear distance,
less substantial than a bank of mist. The far snows of
Albania seemed to drift like cloud.

After the heat of the sand, the water felt cool and
silky. I let myself down into the milky calm, and began
to swim idly along parallel to the shore, towards the
southern arm of the bay. There was the faintest breeze
blowing off the land, its heady mixture of orange-
blossom and pine, sweet and sharp, coming in warm

puffs through the salt smell of the sea. Soon I was nearing the promontory, where white rocks came down to the water, and a grove of pines hung out, shadowing a deep, green pool. I stayed in the sun, turning lazily on my back to float, eyes shut against the brilliance of the sky.

The pines breathed and whispered; the tranquil water made no sound at all . . .

A ripple rocked me, nearly turning me over. As I floundered, trying to right myself, another came, a wash like that of a small boat passing, rolling me in its wake. But I had heard neither oars nor engine; could hear nothing now except the slap of the exhausted ripples against the rock.

Treading water, I looked around me, puzzled and a little alarmed. Nothing. The sea shimmered, empty and calm, to the turquoise and blue of its horizon. I felt downwards with my feet, to find that I had drifted a little further out from shore, and could barely touch bottom with the tips of my toes. I turned back towards the shallows.

This time the wash lifted me clear off my feet, and as I plunged clumsily forward another followed it, tumbling me over, so that I struggled helplessly for a minute, swallowing water, before striking out, thoroughly alarmed now, for shore.

Beside me, suddenly, the water swirled and hissed. Something touched me – a cold, momentary graze along the thigh – as a body drove past me under water . . .

I gave a gasp of sheer fright, and the only reason I

didn't scream was because I gasped myself full of water, and went under. Fighting back, terrified, to the surface, I shook the salt out of my eyes, and looked wildly round – to see the bay as empty as before, but with its surface marked now by the arrowing ripples of whatever sea-creature had brushed by me. The arrow's point was moving fast away, its wake as clear as a vapour-trail across the flat water of the bay. It tore on its way, straight for the open sea . . . then curved in a long arc, heading back . . .

I didn't wait to see what it was. My ignorant mind, panic-stricken, screamed '*Sharks!*' and I struck out madly for the rocks of the promontory.

It was coming fast. Thirty yards off, the surface of the water bulged, swelled, and broke to the curved thrust of a huge, silver-black back. The water parted, and poured off its sides like liquid glass. There was a gasping puff of breath; I caught the glimpse of a dark bright eye, and a dorsal fin cusped like a crescent moon, then the creature submerged again, its wash lifting me a couple of yards forward towards my rock. I found a handhold, clung, and scrambled out, gasping, and thoroughly scared.

It surely wasn't a shark. Hundreds of adventure stories had told me that one knew a shark by the great triangular fin, and I had seen pictures of the terrible jaws and tiny, brutal eye. This creature had breathed air, and the eye had been big and dark, like a dog's – like a seal's, perhaps? But there were no seals in these warm waters, and besides, seals didn't have dorsal fins. A porpoise, then? Too big . . .

Then I had the answer, and with it a rush of relief and delight. This was the darling of the Aegean, 'the lad who lives before the wind', Apollo's beloved, 'desire of the sea', the dolphin . . . the lovely names went rippling by with him, as I drew myself up on to the warm rock in the shade of the pines, clasped my knees, and settled down to watch.

Here he came again, in a great curve, smooth and glistening, dark-backed and light-bellied, and as graceful as a racing yacht. This time he came right out, to lie on the surface watching me.

He was large, as dolphins go, something over eight feet long. He lay rocking gently, with the powerful shoulders waiting curved for the plunge below, and the tail – crescent-shaped, and quite unlike a fish's upright rudder – hugging the water flatly, holding the big body level. The dark-ringed eye watched me steadily, with what I could have sworn was a friendly and interested light. The smooth muzzle was curved into the perpetual dolphin-smile.

Excitement and pleasure made me light-headed. 'Oh, you darling!' I said foolishly, and put out a hand, rather as one puts it out to the pigeons in Trafalgar Square.

The dolphin, naturally, ignored it, but lay there placidly smiling, rocking a little closer, and watching me, entirely unafraid.

So they were true, those stories . . . I knew of the legends, of course – ancient literature was studded with stories of dolphins who had befriended man; and while one couldn't quite accept all the miraculous dolphins of legend, there were also many more recent tales, sworn to with every kind of modern proof. There was the dolphin called Pelorus Jack, fifty years ago in New Zealand, who saw the ships through Cook Straight for twenty years; the Opononi dolphin of the fifties, who entertained the holiday-makers in the bay; the one more recently in Italy, who played with the children near the shore, attracting such large crowds that eventually a little group of business-men from a nearby resort, whose custom was being drawn away, lay in wait for the dolphin, and shot her dead as she came in to play. These, and others, gave the old legends rather more than the benefit of the doubt.

And here, indeed, was the living proof. Here was I, Lucy Waring, being asked into the water for a game. The dolphin couldn't have made it clearer if he'd been carrying a placard on that lovely moon's-horn fin of his. He rocked himself, watching me, then half-turned, rolled, and came up again, nearer still . . .

A stray breeze moved the pines, and I heard a bee go past my cheek, travelling like a bullet. The dolphin arched suddenly away in a deep dive. The sea sucked, swirled, and settled, rocking, back to emptiness.

So that was that. With a disappointment so sharp that it felt like a bereavement, I turned my head to watch for him moving out to sea, when suddenly, not far from my rock, the sea burst apart as if it had been shelled, and the dolphin shot upwards on a steep slant that took him out of the water in a yard-high leap, and down again with a smack of the tail as loud as a cannon-shot. He tore by like a torpedo, to fetch up all standing twenty yards out from my rock, and fix me once again with that bright, humorous eye.

It was an enchanting piece of show-off, and it did the trick. 'All right,' I said softly, 'I'll come in. But if you knock me over again, I'll drown you, my lad, see if I don't!'

I lowered my legs into the water, ready to slide down off the rock. Another bee shot past above me, seawards, with a curious, high humming. Something – some small fish, I supposed – splashed a white jet of water just beyond the dolphin. Even as I wondered, vaguely, what it was, the humming came again, nearer . . . and then another white spurt of water, and a curious thin, curving whine, like singing wire.

I understood then. I'd heard that sound before. These were neither bees nor fish. They were bullets, presumably from a silenced rifle, and one of them had ricocheted off the surface of the sea. Someone was shooting at the dolphin from the woods above the bay.

That I was in some danger from the ricochets myself didn't at first enter my head. I was merely furious, and concerned to do something quickly. There lay the dolphin, smiling at me on the water, while some murderous 'sportsman' was no doubt taking aim yet again . . .

Presumably he hadn't yet seen me in the shadow of the pines. I shouted at the top of my voice: 'Stop that shooting! Stop it at once!' and thrust myself forward into the water.

Nobody, surely, would fire at the beast when there was the chance of hitting me? I plunged straight out

into the sunlight, clumsily breasting the water, hoping
that my rough approach would scare the dolphin away
from the danger.

It did. He allowed me to come within a few feet, but
as I lunged further, with a hand out as if to touch him,
he rolled gently away from me, submerged, and vanished.

I stood breast-deep, watching the sea. Nothing. It
stretched silent and empty towards the tranquil, floating hills of the mainland. The ripples ran back to the
shore, and flattened, whispering. The dolphin had
gone. And the magic had gone with him. This was
only a small – and lonely – bathing-place, above which
waited an unpleasant and frustrated character with a
gun.

I turned to look up at the enclosing cliffs.

The first thing I saw, high up above the bay's centre,
was what must be the upper storeys of the Castello dei
Fiori, rearing their incongruously embattled turrets
against a background of holm-oak and cedar and
Mediterranean cypress. The house was set well back,
so that I could not see the ground-floor windows, but a
wide balcony, or terrace, edged with a stone balustrade, jutted forward right to the cliff's edge over the
bay. From the beach directly below nothing of this
would be visible through the tangle of flowering shrubs
that curtained the steep, broken cliff, but from where I
stood I could see the full length of the balustrade with
its moss-grown statues at the corners, a stone jar or two
full of flowers showing bright against the dark background of cypress, and, a little way back from the

balustrade, a table and chairs set in the shadow of a stone-pine.

And a man standing, half invisible in the shade of the pine, watching me.

A moment's study convinced me that it could not be Sir Julian Gale. This man was too dark, and even from this distance looked quite unfamiliar – too casual in his bearing, perhaps, and certainly too young. The gardener, probably; the one who threw the trespassers over the cliff. Well, if Sir Julian's gardener had the habit of amusing himself with a bit of shooting-practice, it was high time he was stopped.

I was out of the water before even the dolphin could have dived twice, had snatched up shoes and wrap, and was making for a dilapidated flight of steps near the cliff which, I assumed, led up to the terrace.

From above I heard a shout, and looked up. He had come forward to the balustrade, and was leaning over. I could barely see him through the thick screen of hibiscus and bramble, but he didn't look like a Greek, and as I paused, he shouted in English: 'That way, please!' and his arm went out in a gesture towards the southern end of the bay.

I ignored it. Whoever he was – some guest of Julian Gale's, presumably – I was going to have this out with him here and now, while I was hot with temper; not wait until I had to meet him at some polite bun-fight of Phyllida's . . . 'But you really mustn't shoot at dolphins, Mr. Whosit, they do no harm . . .' The same old polite spiel, gone through a thousand times with stupid, trigger-happy men who shot or trapped badgers, otters, kestrels – harmless creatures, killed because some man wanted a walk out with his dog on a fine day. No, this time I was white-hot, and brave with it, and I was going to say my piece.

I went up those steps like a rocket leaving the launching-pad.

They were steep and crooked, and wound up through the thickest of the wood. They skirted the roots of the cliff, flicked up and round thickets of myrtle and summer jasmine, and emerged into a sloping glade full of dappled sunlight.

He was there, looking annoyed, having apparently come down from the terrace to intercept me. I only realised, when I stopped to face him, how very much at a disadvantage I was. He had come down some fifty feet; I had hurtled up a hundred or so. He presumably had a right to be where he was; I had not. He was also minding his own business, which was emphatically none of mine. Moreover, he was fully dressed, and I was in swimming costume, with a wet wrap flying loose round me. I clutched it to me, and fought for breath, feeling angrier than ever, but now this didn't help at all, as I couldn't get a word out.

He said, not aggressively but not politely: 'This is private ground, you know. Perhaps you'd be good enough to leave by the way you came? This only takes you up to the terrace, and then more or less through the house.'

I got enough breath to speak, and wasted neither time nor words. 'Why were you shooting at that dolphin?'

He looked as blank as if I had suddenly slapped his face. 'Why was I what?'

'That was you just now, wasn't it, shooting at the dolphin down in the bay?'

'My dear g—' He checked himself, and said, like someone dealing with a lunatic: 'Just what are you talking about?'

'Don't pretend you don't know! It must have been you! If you're such death on trespassers, who else would be there?' I was panting hard, and my hands were shaking as I clutched the wrap to me clumsily. 'Someone took a couple of pot-shots at it, just a few minutes ago. I was down there, and I saw you on the terrace.'

'I certainly saw a dolphin there. I didn't see you, until you shouted and came jumping out from under the trees. But you must be mistaken. There was no shooting. I'd have been bound to hear it if there was.'

'It was silenced, of course,' I said impatiently. 'I tell you, I was down there when the shots came! D'you think I'd have come running up here for the fun of the thing? They were bullets all right! I know a ricochet when I hear it.'

His brows snapped down at that, and he stared at me frowningly, as if seeing me for the first time as a person, and not just a nuisance to be thrown down the cliff as quickly as possible.

'Then why did you jump into the water near the dolphin?'

'Well, obviously! I wanted to drive it away before it got hurt!'

'But you might have been badly hurt yourself. Don't you know that a bullet ricochets off water the way it does off rock?'

'Of course I do! But I had to do something, hadn't I?'

'Brave girl.' There was a dryness in his voice that brought my cooling temper fizzing to the boil again. I said hotly:

'You don't believe me, do you? I tell you it's true! They *were* shots, and *of course* I jumped in to stop you! I knew you'd have to stop if someone was there.'

'You know,' he said, 'you can't have it both ways. Either I did the shooting, or I don't believe there was any shooting. Not both. You can take your pick. If I were you, I'd choose the second; I mean, it's simply not credible, is it? Even supposing someone wanted to shoot a dolphin, why use a silencer?'

'*I'm* asking *you*,' I said.

For a moment I thought I had gone too far. His lips compressed, and his eyes looked angry. There was a short silence, while he stared at me frowningly, and we measured one another.

I saw a strongly built man of about thirty, carelessly dressed in slacks and a sleeveless Sea Island shirt which exposed a chest and arms that might have belonged to any of the Greek navvies I was to see building the roads with their bare hands and very little more. Like theirs, too, his hair and eyes were very dark. But something at once sensual and sensitive about the mouth contradicted the impression of a purely physical personality; here, one felt, was a man of aggressive impulses, but one who paid for them in his own private coinage.

What impression he was getting of me I hated to think – damp hair, flushed face, half-embarrassed fury, and a damned wrap that kept slipping – but of one thing I could feel pretty sure: at this very moment he was having one of those aggressive impulses of his. Fortunately it wasn't physical . . . yet.

'Well,' he said shortly, 'I'm afraid you'll have to take my word for it. I did not shoot at the beast, with a rifle or a catapult or anything else. Will that do? And now if you'll excuse me, I'll be obliged if you would—'

'Go out by the way I came in? All right. I get the message. I'm sorry, perhaps I was wrong. But I certainly wasn't wrong about the shooting. I don't see any more than you do why anyone should do it, but the fact remains that they did.' I hesitated, faltering now under his indifferent eye. 'Look, I don't want to be any more of a nuisance, but I can't just leave it at that . . . It might happen again . . . Since it wasn't you, have you any idea who it could have been?'

'No.'

'Not the gardener?'

'No.'

'Or the tenant at the Villa Rotha?'

'Manning? On the contrary, if you want help in your protection campaign I suggest you go to the Villa Rotha straight away. Manning's been photographing that beast for weeks. It was he who tamed it in the first place, he and the Greek boy who works for him.'

'Tamed it? Oh . . . I see. Well, then,' I added, lamely, 'it wouldn't be him, obviously.'

He said nothing, waiting, it seemed, with a kind of

neutral patience for me to go. I bit my lip, hesitating miserably, feeling a fool. (Why did one always feel such a fool when it was a matter of kindness – what the more sophisticated saw as sentimentality?) I found that I was shivering. Anger and energy had drained out of me together. The glade was cool with shadows.

I said: 'Well, I imagine I'll see Mr Manning some time soon, and if he can't help, I'm sure my brother-in-law will. I mean, if this is all private land, and the shore as well, then we ought to be able to stop that kind of trespasser, oughtn't we?'

He said quickly: 'We?'

'The people who own the place. I'm Lucy Waring, Phyllida Forli's sister. I take it you're staying with Sir Julian?'

'I'm his son. So you're Miss Waring? I hadn't realised you were here already.' He appeared to be hesitating on the brink of some apology, but asked instead: 'Is Forli at home now?'

'No,' I said shortly, and turned to go. There was a trail of bramble across my shoe, and I bent to disengage it.

'I'm sorry if I was a little abrupt.' His voice had not noticeably softened, but that might have been due to awkwardness. 'We've had rather a lot of bother with people coming around lately, and my father . . . he's been ill, and came here to convalesce, so you can imagine that he prefers to be left to himself.'

'Did I look like an autograph hunter?'

For the first time there was a twitch of amusement. 'Well, no. But your dolphin has been more of an attraction even than my father: the word got round somehow that it was being photographed hereabouts, and then of course the rumour started that a film was being made, so we got a few boat-loads of sightseers coming round into the bay, not to mention stray parties in the woods. It's all been a bit trying. I wouldn't mind, personally, if people wanted to use the beach, if it weren't that they always come armed with transistor radios, and that I cannot stand. I'm a professional musician, and I'm here to work.' He added, dryly: 'And if you're thinking that this gives me the best of reasons for wanting to get rid of the dolphin, I can only assure you again that it didn't occur to me.'

'Well,' I said, 'it seems there's no more to be said, doesn't it? I'm sorry if I interrupted your work. I'll go now and let you get back to it. Goodbye, Mr Gale.'

My exit from the clearing was ruined by the fact that my wrap caught on the bramble, and came clean off me. It took me some three horrible minutes to disentangle it and go.

But I needn't have worried about the threat to my dignity. He had already gone. From somewhere above, and alarmingly near, I heard voices, question and answer, so brief and idle as to be in themselves an insult. Then music, as a wireless or gramophone let loose a flood of weird atonal chords on the still air.

I could be sure I was already forgotten.

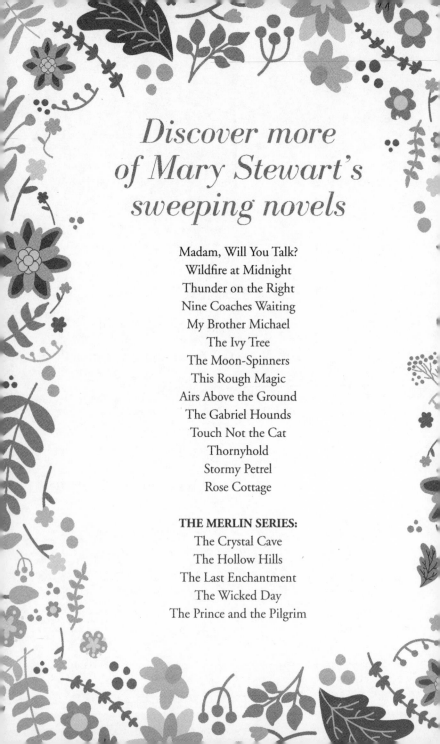

Discover more
of Mary Stewart's
sweeping novels

Madam, Will You Talk?
Wildfire at Midnight
Thunder on the Right
Nine Coaches Waiting
My Brother Michael
The Ivy Tree
The Moon-Spinners
This Rough Magic
Airs Above the Ground
The Gabriel Hounds
Touch Not the Cat
Thornyhold
Stormy Petrel
Rose Cottage

THE MERLIN SERIES:
The Crystal Cave
The Hollow Hills
The Last Enchantment
The Wicked Day
The Prince and the Pilgrim